Uncaged Stories:
Short stories and excerpts of the creative writing of incarcerated men

Uncaged Stories:
Short stories and excerpts of the creative writing of incarcerated men

Rahsaan Thomas, Jeffrey Little, Eric Curtis and Julian Glenn Padgett

Plus a few chapters from each author's upcoming books, including Fight to Breathe: the life story of two-time Heavyweight Champion Shannon Briggs written by Rahsaan Thomas

First Printing: 2014

ISBN # 978-0-9913728-1-2

Self-published by Rahsaan Thomas
SQSP T99595
San Quentin, CA 94974

uncagedstories@gmail.com

Dedication

This book is dedicated to my son Nicholas who made it possible for men in cages to self-publish. Thanks to Photographer Peter Merts for providing the cover photo and Zoe for teaching us how to be better writers. Special thanks also to Pop, Leslie, Michelle, Pattie, Rasta Von, Crystal, Tyrell, Shannon and Stan who support this vision.
-Rahsaan

Contents

One Bad Apple

14 year old Billy didn't think the small gun brandished at him looked real. It's matted midnight black finish resembled a plastic cap pistol he possessed when he was seven. Besides, where would a fellow 14 year old get a real gun?

Billy didn't have access to such weapons so he didn't believe the gat being waived at him and his 11 year old brother, Jimmy, was real.

"I'm not playing with you! Run your ring or else!" threatened a hoodie clad young thug. Billy still didn't take the gun-waving jacker serious. Although a cowl-like cloth partially hid Beam's identity, it was obviously him. He lived two blocks away. How could he be robbing someone he knows?

"Stop playing and get out of my face," Billy defiantly responded, not believing he was being robbed for real. Born in 1970 and raised up in Howard Housing Projects, he had heard guns fire before, heard of neighborhood kids being shot, but had never had a revolver pointed at him. So he wasn't willing to relinquish the gold pinky ring inherited from his murdered father to this baby thug. Being about a foot taller than his 4'11 assailant gave Billy the confidence to ignore the miniature goon from down the block with the fake gun.

Beam was dead serious though. Without further warning, he aimed at Billy and pulled the trigger on a very real .32 caliber revolver. At speeds faster than the human eye, its cylinder spun lining up a bullet with the gun's hammer. Its metal spike-like tip hit the back of the bullet's copper casing right in the spot designated to cause the gunpowder inside to explode, launching a deadly projectile. Death or great bodily injury was headed directly towards Billy.

But while Billy stood frozen in shock, his little brother pushed him out of the way, yelling "RUN!" So Billy ran and ran, as the sound of multiple shots could be heard following. The fear of being hit in the back by multiple bullets inspired his track-star's speed burst.

The brick walls of his projects faced outwards, like fort walls. They circled a court yard, surrounded by entrances to each building. Billy ran around a side pathway, all the way to his building before looking back to realize that Jimmy wasn't behind him.

He had to go back – back to where he was almost killed. Big brothers are supposed to save little brothers, not the other way around. Police wouldn't get there in time, couldn't get there in time because it was probably already too late.

At a slower pace, Billy cautiously retraced his steps to the scene on Glenmore Avenue. He went down the dirty concrete pathway wishing his Todd One sweat suit was made of bullet proof material. A Street light illuminated the gunfire's tally. The artificial light held the darkening evening sky in abeyance and revealed Jimmy lying out on the ground in a pool of his own blood.

New emotions overran any fear of Beam. Anger, sadness, and disappointment at getting his little bro shot consumed him. With tears pouring down his face, he kneeled down and held Jimmy until the cops and an ambulance showed up.

A pretty Hispanic female paramedic cut Jimmy's shirt and pants off, revealing several bullet wounds. Small round holes overflowing with blood, like flooded wells, peppered his shoulder, stomach and upper thigh area. Jimmy was critically wounded over a hundred dollar piece of jewelry.

While he was rushed to the hospital, a police detective asked Billy some questions. The interview which sought to get necessary information required to locate and apprehend the guilty party felt like an interrogation. "Who shot your little brother? Why would a 14 year old shoot an 11 year old? Where'd you get that ring? How long have you been selling drugs? Where is your momma?" Meanwhile, a cop just arriving at the scene mumbled something about N-H-I.

Billy and Jimmy are latchkey kids. Billy watches over Jimmy until their mother returns from work. She was at her place of employment when the attempt to murder her sons went down. Billy was taken to the precinct to await her arrival.

There he overheard what NHI means. A uniformed officer jokingly asked a colleague, "Was the shooting another No Humans Involved case?" N-H-I. Jimmy certainly appeared human to Billy as his blood stained the concrete.

No arrest was made although Beam hung around the neighborhood. The police did the old go-through-the-motions routine.

Detectives knocked on Beam's door to arrest him, but he wasn't home. After that, they fell back, being more concerned about other cases. Billy was given a card with a number to call when Beam was spotted. They actually expected Billy to call the police and hope they arrived before Beam murdered the key witness against him.

Billy decided otherwise while watching television. On the screen, Charles Bronson was taking vigilant action against two street punks in a dark alley. They were dressed in black leather biker outfits and were welding knives. Bronson had a .44 revolver and the determination to punish them for prior acts of pure evil. When the thugs made their move, Bronson aired them both out. Billy cheered as each blast hit the bad men. He hoped to do the same to Beam.

It turns out getting a gat wasn't that hard for a 14 year old. Dope fiends will sell anything to anybody for little or nothing. With a weekend's paper-route money, Billy bought a .25 caliber Raven Arms semi-automatic with seven bullets.

As soon as the evening sun set, Billy dressed in all blue and went Beam hunting. He fearlessly headed to Beam's block. There, in front of a bodega he saw him.

From 15 feet away, Beam saw Billy approaching with a gun in hand and tried to draw his own. POW, pow, pow, the little .25 erupted, beating Beam to the punch. One of the three shots hit Beam directly in his heart.

However, a person shot thru the heart can still function for up to 30 seconds. Although Beam was literally a dead teen walking, he used his last moments on earth to take down Billy with him. Bam, bam, his .32 responded. Billy was hit in the chest as well.

As Billy's life drained away, he had an epiphany. His mother's warnings popped into his head. "If you live by the sword, you will die by the sword" and "Never argue with fools because people far away can't tell the difference." The meaning of those words came too late, as Billy died at the scene.

As the same police and detectives arrived, the NHI comments continued. They didn't see how their indifference created that situation. They didn't see a God-fearing newspaper boy desperate to take some power back and avenge his brother. All they saw was the aftermath of two teens who gunned each other down in the street like dogs.

Jimmy survived but came home from the hospital with premeditated, nonmetal-detectable thoughts of guns and violence on his mind. At 11 years of age, he was ready to take up arms. In just a few days, one bad apple spoiled a whole bunch.

Mental Battlefields

His first enlistment resulted in a tense week of prolonged anxiety over battles he didn't fight in. Naval officer, Kamal Woods was on an aircraft carrier during Desert Storm. The six-foot four St. Louis native recalled the intense fear that shocked him into action every time the alarm sounded. From wherever he was, whatever he was doing, the loud screeching shrill and flashing strobe lights demanded manning battle stations in full war gear. No missiles or attacks ever reached his ship just off the shore of Kuwait. However, the mere possibility that each alert could mean fighting for his very life racked his nerves.

It felt like he barely escaped the Grimm Reaper's clutches each time the "All clear!" was signaled. Helicopters loaded with men not so lucky heightened the harsh realities that awaited the war participants. Each man who lost a limb or those who were no longer breathing demonstrated the fragile nature of human beings and how easy it is to die. He didn't want to lose his life so far from home. To meet his end in foreign waters, without relatives around, would be a horrible way to die. Woods feared dying for and with strangers.

Not knowing how long the war would last, he survived it by telling himself, "The ship will be back seaside soon." Just like Dorothy's mantra in the Wizard of Oz, "There's no place like home," it seemingly worked because the war was over in ten days and Woods made it home safely.

When homecoming came, it wasn't soon enough. He was welcomed with a cooked meal of soul food by his mother. However, as he kissed her on the forehead, she could sense differences between the boy who left and the person who returned. The suspicious look on her son's face whenever there was an unexpected noise; the way he kept fidgeting; and his reserved demeanor especially were all new to her. The signs subtly vibrated from his psyche. Naval officer Woods made it back to St. Louis, but Kamal didn't.

Woods returned angry, solemn, tense and jumpy. He was angry with himself for being scared of what never happened. How could he explain to anyone that a war in which he never had to fight had shaken him to his very core? Yet he couldn't help snapping into battle mode whenever he heard a siren – a common occurrence in the Lou. This made him quiet, depressed, angry and tense.

He couldn't function in society. The reasons weren't logical; they were psychological, but also overbearing. He couldn't maintain relationships or employment and so ended up being 're-enlisted.'

He was back to the regimens and horrible conditions of naval life. First there was the physical, then written test called ASVAB to determine job placement. Back to the tasteless grub and double bunks crammed into small hot uncomfortable spaces. Back to those wool blankets that made him itch. Back to long lines to use a carwash-type shower in the open. Back to wearing blues and boots all the time, and back to taking orders from younger men. He had to keep telling himself, "The ship will be back seaside soon" to trick his mind through each day.

He always looked forward to two things and both were from home. One was the care packages he was allowed to receive every 90 days. His mom would send all kinds of food, from beef summer sausages to Hershey Cookies and Cream candy bars that were a great comfort. They gave him a needed break from the crappy government chow. Then there was the mail. He loved hearing about and from home, even though he didn't like writing back. Each package, each correspondence, brought him to port for a few minutes at a time – at least in his mind.

On one particular day, he had just left his quarters when the siren started sounding. As fear electrified him, he quickly surveyed his surroundings for signs of a real attack. He spotted foreigners with shaved bald heads overrunning the ship. This time the enemy was upon him and he could not avoid being in the midst of combat.

Impulses to fight or take flight surged through his nervous system. His comrades were equally divided between the two extremes. Some ran. Others stood their ground against the surprise attack. At first he stood there, frozen in shock by paralyzing fear as he watched a fellow midshipman being attacked by four hostiles using knives. Then greater fears of being next, of allowing a brother-in-arms to get killed, and of being labeled a coward, kicked in and made him angry. That anger boiled into intense rage which overcame his fear and catapulted him into fight mode.

He charged the line of scrimmage, armed with only years of unused training. The four enemies hacking at the midshipman had their backs to Woods. He took them from behind with a flying kick that caught one square in the back, sending him crashing into another and causing them both to fall like dominos. The other two stopped stabbing the sailor and turned to face the element that surprised them. Woods greeted the closest one with a standard military taught chop to his throat, leaving him gasping for air. The others wouldn't be so easy.

As the last standing bald-headed tan complexioned attacker waived a long bladed knife, his buddies made it back to their feet. Regrouped, the three spread out, cutting off any avenue of escape and closed in on Woods. He steadied himself to face the losing odds, fear returning, as they approached in unison. His fellow sailor was too wounded to help and no others were in the immediate area. Woods had bitten off more than he could chew.

As the three combatants advanced, Woods backed away until cornered. They were all slashing at him with their mini-swords, as he stayed just out of reach, but with nowhere else to go, Woods was in trouble.

As they were about to kill him, a mini-14 rifle round blew the brains of the lead attacker out. Other shots followed, along with orders shouted over a megaphone to get down. A squad of Naval Master-at-Arms in full battle gear rushed onto the scene. Tear gas exploded. Choking thick white smoke invaded the air. Woods had to get down or risk being hit by friendly fire. The bald-headed enemies were being taken down all round him. Woods was being saved.

Then one of the naval officers came over and started roughly cuffing Woods' wrist. As he began to protest, a moment of clarity made it through the fog in his mind. He noticed a Goon Squad patch on the arm of the Correctional Officers manhandling him. As his mental vision cleared, he saw the bars making up the cells in that block. He wasn't on a ship at sea, he was in prison.

Then the moment passed and his mind went back out to sea. Woods could only handle serving the rest of his natural life in prison for murder in small doses at a time. He had to tell himself, had to believe that he was only out at sea and would be seaside soon.

Respect My Gangster

It was a perfect day for playing basketball. 80 degrees with a gentle breeze that flowed through the projects attempting to keep everyone cool. The lite wind carried the lyrics of Jay Z and Alicia Keys singing about growing up in New York. "...concrete jungle it's made if, there's nothing you can't do..."

The music came from the radio of one of many teens in attendance at the Hole in Van Dyke Projects. Huge concrete steps led from ground level to a full basketball court, forming a square hole and doubling as bleachers. Guys and gals sat watching the game being played. Hot chicks were chilling in short-shorts and baby t-tops, showing off paths to pleasure.

It was just a pickup game. Out of habit, the teams still formed along project lines. Five guys from Van Dyke against five from Tilden Projects, which was just across the street. Jordan sneakers, Under Armor Gear and other high fashion masked the poverty of the competing athletes.

The game went to 21 and Van Dyke had the ball, down four at 15 to Tilden's 19. Johnny, an 18-year old running point, dribbled the ball down court, determined to go coast to coast. Gangsta, a 21-year old who just came home from a robbery beef, cut off his lane. Without missing a beat, Johnny bounced the basketball through Gangster's legs, spun around him and recovered the ball past Gangsta. When another Tilden player came over to help defend Johnny, he was too late. Johnny was already flying thru the air for the slam dunk, making the score 17-19.

The crowd went crazy. "Ooh! In your face!"

"He burnt Gangsta!"

"Highlight reel!" and other pro Van Dyke chants were heard.

Johnny's girl Maria was watching from a seat on the steps. She jumped up in excitement, proud of her man. The Puerto Rican and Black bombshell's firm c-cups bounced with her movement. Johnny blew her a kiss as he got back on defense. He couldn't wait to see her after the game.

Rambo got really mad. He decided to return the favor. The ball went inbounds to him. He did a crossover and went past Johnny. However, Johnny recovered quickly enough to swat the ball from behind. Johnny completed the steal and went towards the rack. Gangsta got in the way just in time to get dunked on.

The rim and chain-link net rattled as Johnny's sneakers returned to the terra firma. His eyes smiled in a celebratory glee along with his lips.

Gangsta didn't share his joy and responded by pushing Johnny. Although they were both 6-foot-2 inches tall, Johnny was 3 years younger and 30 pounds of muscle lighter. Johnny didn't back down though, he pushed Gangsta back, asking, "What's your problem?"

"My problem is you fagot ass nigger!"

"The hell with you man!"

"What! Suck my dick punk!"

Everyone paused as those dangerous words hung heavily in the air. Teammates who were coming over to break up the brewing beef stopped in their tracks, as if the conflict had already gone past the point of no return.

How or when the phrase "Suck my dick!" became a life and death challenge when said to another man wasn't known to Johnny. Maybe it started in prison. Rape was common in New York penitentiaries back in the days. You couldn't allow yourself to be disrespected like that. It would make you appear weak and weak men got their manhood taken. So any form of sex playing wasn't tolerated. Johnny had made it to 18 without ever being locked up. Yet he knew from others who had that you just don't let another man say that to you unless you were a chump.

Gangsta knew exactly what those words meant. He had been in and out of prison since he was 16. He knew the exact implications when he filled the air with the declaration of war.

There effect vibrated thru the atmosphere like a loud smack. The crowd held their breath in anticipation of a response. Johnny had to act. There was no choice, the streets were watching.

He lashed out with a left jab. Gangsta sidestepped the expected punch easily and delivered an overhand right that knocked Johnny down. Before Johnny could recover his senses, Gangsta kicked him in the mouth. Blood flew from lips badly busted against his own teeth.

He could feel that his incisor tooth was loose. Another kick left Johnny out cold on the blacktop. His face sat in a pool of his own blood and sweat. Gangsta spit on Johnny, yelled, "Dunk on that," and mobbed off.

No one else got involved. The tension ran thick between the rival projects. However, it was a one on one fight. Had anyone else jumped in, there would have been a melee. Since the insult and actions were personal, it wasn't anybody else's business to handle. Gangsta was allowed to leave Van Dyke with his boys despite Maria yelling, "Get them!"

Johnny regained consciousness while being carried by teammates into building 393. Kaborn held him up from one side while BI from the other. Johnny's ears were ringing and his vision was reduced to a narrow straight-ahead angle. Maria followed behind cursing in Spanish. Johnny's head hurt as much as his pride. He had been publicly humiliated in the worst ways --dissed, knocked out, stomped, and spit on in front everybody including his girl. He could barely figure out where he was past the drum beating inside his hurting head, but one thought clearly rode that beat--revenge.

"I'm going to kill him," Johnny said aloud more to himself than his boys.

"You damn sure have to do something. It can't end like that," said Kaborn, a livewire from the third floor.

"Aye, don't listen to him. You start your scholarship playing for Syracuse this fall. Let it go," pleaded Maria.

"Let it go? Let it go? How can I? That freaking hater started this! He had no right getting at me like that. Plus he stomp me out and spat on me in front of everybody."

"Who cares what these losers think! Kill them with success. Go to school and never look back," Maria responded.

"This is my neighborhood. I'm always going to come back to it. I have to return here. I can't hide at school forever. I can't let him get away with this," Johnny declared while barely holding back tears of anger and frustration.

"He's right Maria," Kaborn added.

"Don't be stupid. Why should he throw his life away over that loser!" Maria told Kaborn.

"You have to be alive to be successful and these streets eat weaklings alive. He has to respond!" Kaborn fired back.

"I have to do what I have to do," Johnny agreed.

The next day Gangsta was walking past Van Dyke as if he ruled it. His Jesus piece laced in cloudy diamonds, on a thick white gold Cuban link chain reflected sunrays. It bounced off his chiseled brown skin as he glided down Dumont Avenue in board daylight like a King. His naked upper torso showed off a collage of artwork in green ink. The tattoos ranged from guns and skulls to his baby momma's name. Iceberg jeans sagged, revealing the waistband of Polo boxers. Timberland boots were worn without socks. The confidence of having just knocked another man out completed his outfit. He was feeling tall.

Jimmy was looking out the window of the bedroom he shared with a younger brother. From there he saw Gangsta and hatred filled his heart with rage. Gangsta was adding insult to injury by prancing by Van Dyke like that. The sight set Johnny's soul afire. He didn't have a gun and couldn't borrow one before Gangsta got away. So thinking through a mind befogged by anger, he grabbed a kitchen utensil and ran down 13 flights of stairs to pursue his enemy.

Johnny crept up from behind with a huge butcher knife, breathing too hard to speak. Gangsta was oblivious to death approaching. Gangsta strolled to the corner without a care in the world. Without hesitation Johnny blasted the disrespectful man in his neck. Blood cascaded like a waterfall as Johnny removed the blade. Gangsta's confidence abandoned him once the steel went through his esophagus. Gangsta fell to the ground screaming and holding his neck, while Johnny coldly walked away.

Several people saw what happened from the busy corner of Dumont and Mother Gaston. Some gaped at the horror scene. Others avert their eyes, signaling they didn't want to be involved. An old lady walked on by as if there wasn't a man bleeding to death on the concrete before her. Altogether at least 20 people were around. Most raised in Brooklyn wouldn't cooperate with the authorities, but with that many witnesses the police were sure to hear something.

Johnny didn't care. He wanted the world to know he stabbed Gangsta. He wanted everybody to know never to humiliate him again.

He walked to his building with his head held high. Everyone moved out his path.

An hour later the police showed up in force. Two detectives and six uniform cops came to Johnny's 13th floor apartment. The lead cop pounded on the door. The officers behind him had their guns drawn. Seven Glocks awaits any hostile movement. "Police, open up!" one yelled.

Johnny calmly answered the door. Dressed in a navy blue Sean John sweat suit, he was ready to be taken to jail. As soon as he opened the metal door, the cops rushed in. They grabbed him roughly and took him to the ground. He didn't put up a fight and was apprehended fast.

The cops picked Johnny up and marched him out. "You're going away for a long time," the lead detective said. Johnny remained quiet as he was taken towards the elevators. His mother came out into the hallway screaming, "Where are you taking my son?" already knowing the answer. "Don't say nothing Johnny, I'll be down there," she told her boy with tears riding the curve of her cheekbones.

Not all the police could fit in one elevator so five rode down with Johnny while the rest waited for the other one. Johnny felt like he was descending into hell as the cables lowered the car to the lobby. Maria was standing there waiting to ride up when her man came out shackled and escorted. She had already heard what happened and was racing to see him. She started sobbing uncontrollably as she realized she wasn't in time.

Johnny had to detach himself from emotions. He couldn't deal with the fact that he was facing long imprisonment over a basketball game gone bad. He had to remain hard. He was quiet as the police asked their questions in an interrogation room at the precinct. Even his own thoughts were silent as he kept his mind numb.

After the failed interrogation, Johnny was subjected to the booking process. He was taken to an empty cell and ordered to strip. Johnny complied, handing over each item of clothing to the officer. He felt uncomfortable undressing in front of other men, but knew he had no choice.

As he stood butt naked, the officer gave further instructions. "Lift up your nuts." Johnny held up his scrotum. "Good. Now open your mouth wide and run your fingers around your mouth." Johnny complied with the command to put the same fingers that just held his balls into his mouth. "Now lift up your arms. Okay, turn around, bend over and spread your butt cheeks." Johnny sighed then turned around, bent over and pulled his butt cheeks apart while the officer looked up his anus with a flashlight for contraband. The degrading process seemed to take forever as cold air conditioning caused goose bumps on his arms. He didn't feel very manly.

Another cop took Johnny to be photographed and printed. Johnny had to stand holding a sign with his name and some numbers on it for the camera man. He didn't say cheese. Afterwards he was ordered to relax his hand while a female officer put thick black ink on his fingertips. She then rolled them onto index like cards and then a small scanner. Finally Johnny was put back in a cell and given a brown paper sack.

He was starving. The process had taken long and he hadn't eaten before stabbing Gangsta. He sat on his bunk and opened the bag to be disappointed by its contents. There was some kind of sandwich, with a mystery meat that smelled and tasted horrible. One bite and Johnny was gagging. Dinner ended up being an apple, one chocolate cookie and some water. He went to sleep hungry on the thin mattress over the small metal bed.

Johnny awoke the next day to a heckling cop. "You're really done now. Your buddy died. Now the charge is murder," said the fat lead detective.

He was a killer now. Top of the food chain. Someone no one would disrespect. Johnny's amazing basketball talent would go wasted on a prison yard. However he got what he wanted. He would have the ultimate respect—in prison.

Institutionalized: Part III

A poem by Rahsaan Thomas

All men are created equal, true indeed, but the constitution still ain't up to speed. 3/5 of a man, they enslaved us, 2008 -- 1/3 they incarcerate us; It's like they hate us. N.H.I – they don't care about you or I, poverty and skin color why, they just let us die. NO HUMANS INVOLVED, the case may never get solved. Revolvers revolve; and now one is pointed at me; police ain't ever where they're supposed to be. While they do lunch; one bad apple spoils a whole bunch; shots go off; my little brother goes down; he looks human to me, as his blood splatters the ground. We got good grades in schools; neither of us carried a tool; but when you're young and Black; that's that; all the police feel they need to know; jaded to how the streets go; they let the heats blow; now I'm infected, 'cause my hood ain't protected. Loopholes opened by the NRA make it easy to get guns to me; armed and ready, it won't happen again; not to my next of kin. But sure enough, two tried; and one died; by the gun in my hand; and my determination to take a stand; but am I standing in the wrong place? Racing in the wrong race? Surviving gang banger caught with the gun in the palm of his hand; and they let him go like he is part of the plan, part of the Klan while they life the one who, if given a squeal, would help up-lift his people; meanwhile, they found both of their guns. In Iraq, they found none, I killed that man; that's square buzz, but if it wasn't self-defense, then what the hell is?

Amanda

"God, I hate my life!" I whispered vehemently. But as usual, no one paid any attention to me.

As I stood in line waiting for a bank teller and for the next unknown event to take place in my life, the disgusting memory of my wife fucking two men floated to the surface of my mind. My heart began to thump like an African drum as adrenaline and hatred pumped through my veins, causing my mouth to go dry and my lungs to suck air violently into its fleshy cavern.

At that point in my existence, I wanted to destroy myself, to stop myself from breathing; so that I would be placed in a soft bed of dirt and would sleep in dormancy. Fact is, I'd been betrayed by the one person I'd loved and respected; and now, I was exhausted with my life and had taken up bank robbery as a means to an end.

Then I met Amanda.

Well, I didn't actually meet her, but I learned her name by reading the name-tag pinned to her blouse. There were other people standing in line with me as she approached, but she stopped directly in front of me, as though responding to some sort of beacon.

She looked me up and down, openly measuring and taking in my countenance with her dazzling smoke-grey eyes, which sparkled with a hint of mischief and a flash of anger.

"Anything I can do for you?" she asked softly. Her smile was beautiful; it radiated from her heart and out through her eyes; yet she seemed to look through me and into the darkest part of my soul.

I was mesmerized and my speech was temporarily disabled.

"Can I help you?" she asked again, amusement dancing in her expression as she gently touched my wrist. Her voice was feminine and alluring, captivating me within her clutches, and I didn't want to be freed.

I felt charged with the heat that burned hotly within my being, filling me with a corrupt desire for this caramel-complexioned woman, with long black tresses. The combination of her voice and her fiery touch, teased my sexual appetite and I suddenly wanted to be her everything – her man, her savior, and her god.

Amanda

These thoughts rushed obscenely through my head right before I replied, "No, I'm good."

"Are you sure?" she asked in a melodic timbre that seemed to melt me like hot butter.

"Yes, I'm sure" I said, unable to look her in the eyes.

When she walked away, my eyes followed her, taking in the voluptuousness of her perfectly shaped butt and the strength of her legs. I luxuriated in the scent of her wafting perfume, *Chanel No. 5*, which overloaded my senses and made my hunger for Amanda grow to a depth I'd never experienced.

Amanda soon disappeared from sight and that's when depression set in. For just a brief moment, she had been the sunlight that chased the shadows from my soul.

I knew Amanda and I could never be. I was a dirty, unscrupulous man who was also reckless and uncaring, and that made me dangerous to myself and to her. And Amanda was the sort of woman who would never soil herself with the likes of broken individuals such as I was.

I touched the small pistol at my back and decided I'd rob a different bank.

Later that evening, I found myself anxious for no apparent reason and could not get Amanda off my mind.

Wanting to be alone, I drove to Horton Plaza and parked in a lot that was high enough to give me an exquisite view of the city and a humbling look at the dark sky with its twinkling stars.

Just as I shut off my vehicle's engine, a man, a woman and four children, in tow, noisily passed by my car. The youngest child stopped, waved, and gave me a heart-warming smile.

I offered a weak smile in return.

Fifteen minutes later, while I sat on the surrounding wall trying to get drunk, I heard a woman's scream – it was filled with fear and, strangely, it sounded familiar.

I removed a *.357* from my waist and cautiously made way toward the sounds of violence. As I ducked between cars, I came upon a sight that unnerved me, and suddenly wanted to kill someone to become a hero.

Two men were attempting to throw Amanda over the cement wall and would have sent her plummeting to her death, *50* feet down.

"Get your hands off that woman and step the fuck back!" I shouted. Shooting two assholes to rescue the woman who'd stolen my heart was a win-win course of action for me.

One man spun on me and was reaching for his weapon, when a deafening boom from my Desert Eagle split the night air sending two hot rounds into his chest.

Just as the man slumped dead onto the pavement, Amanda fiercely shoved the second guy over the retaining wall and he screamed falling to his death.

Breathing heavily, Amanda ran to where I stood and hugged me. Even under duress, she was breathtakingly beautiful.

"What the fuck was that all about?" I asked, not fully comprehending the fact that I'd just killed a man.

"Do you have a car nearby?" Amanda asked, ignoring my question.

"Yeah" I replied evenly. "Follow me."

We ran to my car, a 2011 CTS Ragtop. Once inside, Amanda turned to me and said, "I live in La Jolla. If you take me home, it will be well worth your while. Those men were trying to kidnap me and I need to inform my father about the plans his enemies have put into play."

"I'll get you to your father," I assured her.

As I pulled out of the parking garage, police cruisers passed us, heading into the pit of hell.

I was a quarter-mile away from the scene of death when Amanda clutched her stomach and said, "Please, pull over! I think I'm going to be sick!"

I pulled over to the curb and Amanda nearly jumped from my vehicle.

Then she stoop up straight and her expression became evil and grotesque as she removed from her purse an electronic device, followed by a wicked-looking gun.

"Toss your gun out of the car," she commanded. When I hesitated, she fired a round into the headrest of my seat.

I threw out my gun and said, "I saved your life and this is how you fucking repay me?"

"Yes, and unfortunately you just blew up Horton Plaza and killed hundreds of people, including innocent children."

I stared in horror as she pressed buttons on her device and, seconds later, a big fireball lit up the sky – and then I felt the rumble of the explosions.

"What the hell did you just do?" I screamed at this strange woman, as I thought about the little girl who'd waved at me.

"I've just given you a reason to live, mother-fucker," Amanda said wickedly.

Then she shot me.

A Father's Dying Revenge

I would probably categorize the day I met Jessie Parks, a little over nineteen years ago, as one of the worst days of my life. That day, I lost the right to be called a citizen of the United States. I stood before a beautiful, dark-haired Hispanic woman, who ceremoniously stripped me of the one thing I held dear to my heart: my freedom.

"I hereby sentence you to a term of 48 months" the woman was saying to me. "You will be remanded to the custody of the Federal Bureau of Prisons...." Suddenly, everything went black.

As I retrieved my mind from the atmosphere, I realized I was no longer in the courtroom but found myself in a small holding cell with four other men. Out of the five inmates present, only one of us smiled.

I could feel myself becoming angry as I stared at the dark-skinned black man with the pearl white teeth and rugged good looks. While the rest of us wore gloomy faces, this stranger had the nerve to grin.

My mouth suddenly acted on impulse. I blurted out, "Hey! How much time did the Feds drop on you?"

Several heads turned in my direction but it was clear to three of the men that I wasn't speaking to them.

"Hey!" I said a little more forcibly, still failing to communicate with my brain. "How much did honorable Gonzales hit you with?"

The man who I addressed slowly turned his head and looked directly at me with eyes that pierced straight to the core of my soul. With a voice as deep as Barry White's, the man said to me, "My name is not 'Hey' it's Jessie Parks and that woman who you referred to as honorable, hit me with 96 months for Bank Robbery. What about you? How much did she knock you out for?"

I smiled because I was made to feel at ease and I introduced myself. "Name is Terrence Carter, but everyone calls me T.C. And to answer your question, Gonzales broke me off 48 months for gun possession on a military base." And just like that, Jessie and I became friends.

As luck would have it, Jessie and I were sent out of San Diego, up the coast to an old Federal Prison, situated close to the Vandenberg

A Father's Dying Revenge

Air-Force Base. A prison known for its eruptions of violence and fatalities: the United States Penitentiary, Lompoc.

The prison was as formidable and scary-looking as any within the country. As I stood on the outside of the three fences, equipped with rows upon rows of razor wire, looking at the structure that would be my home for the next four years, my stomach sank and my bowels felt like they were about to give way to the fear that suddenly gripped and suffocated me.

"Calm down man," Jessie's soothing voice said. "Ain't nothing but another cage. Do your own time, mind your business and before you know it, your time will be up and you'll be back on the bricks, chasin' some honeys. Besides, I got your back."

It was 1992, I was 23 years of age and my family had temporarily disowned me because of the trouble I'd gotten myself into. Somehow, Jessie picked up on that fact and without my asking, he took up the slack, making sure I had what I needed.

During the time I got to know Jessie, I received the honor of meeting Tonya, his son's mother, and his son, Deonte. The child was a beautiful, mixed boy, with bright inquisitive eyes. He was the love and the strength of Jessie's life.

Jessie loved that child more than anyone else on the planet. He told me one day, "I'm happy because I believe that no matter what happens in my life, my son will always love me because he is me."

It was April 22, Deonte's fourth birthday and as with every other birthday; Jessie would call to speak to his son. But this year was different. Thirty seconds into their conversation, something went wrong.

I don't know what Tonya said, but Jessie suddenly exploded. His words had gotten so loud that other inmates stopped and listened as he berated Tonya, using every expletive he could think of to degrade her. Jessie then ended their conversation by threatening to kill her.

It's a known fact that men and women in prison, get angry with their loved ones, and say things that are in no way to be taken seriously. Yet, when I looked in Jessie's eyes as he hung up the telephone, I believed that Jessie would kill if pushed. I had the sense that he'd just been shoved hard.

Needless to say, Jessie never got the chance to speak with Deonte again, and as time continued it left its mark on him. Jessie began to change, both mentally and physically. For one, he was no longer the ally I once depended upon and he didn't smile much. We barely spoke and when we did, the only thing Jessie would speak about was how he missed his son, and how he couldn't wait to get out of prison to make things right.

One day, with tears of regret, Jessie said to me, "I know I ain't been the best father a man can be, but I love my son and I did the best I know how. To know my son now hates me because of a lie inspired by his mother, I feel like I'm fighting a battle that I will never win. And now, I feel like the pain of losing my child's love has finally outweighed my love for him. I have to fight back and make Tonya feel how losing your child rips at your heart and soon makes you feel nothing but hate. I want her to know."

It would be years before I understood the velocity of Jessie's statement.

It was April 22, 2011, and I'd been out of prison for a number of years. I was working at N.A.S.S.C.O, one of San Diego's famous ship building yards as a welder. Because of my skill, I earned nearly forty dollars an hour. I lived in a big, four bedroom and was happily married to a beautiful Colombian woman, with three boys of my own. I loved my family very much. They were simply my life support. Without them, I could not breathe nor could I exist.

I guess the only reason I was thinking of Jessie at all, was because of the date. I remembered that April 22 was Deonte's birthday, and today was that day. Deonte would be 20 years old. I smiled to myself as I remembered the bright eyed, handsome little boy that was full of life and who at one time, had loved his father as though Jessie was the only man on the planet.

My wife was in the kitchen preparing dinner, and I was sitting on the couch, feeding my youngest son, when my program was interrupted with an alarming story. A man had just shot and killed another man down in the courtyard of the Civic Center, in downtown San Diego.

The story caught my attention and I turned up the volume. I watched as a helicopter with a camera moved closer to the murder scene and what I saw next, nearly took my breath away. My eyes immediately welled up and tears poured down my face as I watched the scene play out before me.

There was Jessie Parks, sitting on the ground, covered with Deonte's blood as he cradled his son's head in his lap. A pistol remained in Jessie's right hand, and police were closing in with their weapons drawn.

As the camera zoomed in on Jessie's face, he looked towards the helicopter, and blew his own brains out.

I jumped as I witnessed the horrific event play out before my eyes. My heart poured out in tears for Jessie and Deonte, because I knew them and I knew what Jessie had gone through. Yet, I had done nothing to assist him when he needed help the most. I'd let him down and if it hadn't been for Jessie, I would have lost my mind during my first year of being in prison.

"Baby, are you all right?" My wife asked as she entered the room.

"No, I'm not" I replied. "Something really bad just happened on the news." And as I looked at her, then back at my son, a creepy notion entered my mind. I knew that there was no way I would allow myself to be tortured like Tonya had done to Jessie, forcing him to believe there was no other way he could be with his only son.

When was the Last Time?

This morning, when Lonnie came from taking his shower, I walked into his arms and his embrace felt like he had all the love in the world for me. However, for the life of me, I couldn't remember the last time he said, "I love you."

The day was nice and warn and Lonnie said, "You know baby, we haven't been anywhere in quite some time, and there's a fair close by, would you like to go?"

"That sounds like fun and I'll go on one condition."

"Oh now we have conditions" Lonnie said.

I folded my arms across my chest and just looked at him.

"Okay okay, what is it?" he asked.

"That you leave your phone at home."

"My phone? But what if I'm needed?"

"You're always needed", I said, "You're needed by the whole world it seems, and right now I need you to leave that phone here."

Reluctantly he took his phone out and turned it off. When he put it back in his pocket, I stomped my foot and crossed my arms again. "Lonnie please, I want this day to be about you and me."

"I thought that's what I was trying to do?"

"Lonnie it's Saturday, I think the world can survive one day without you."

"But…"

"No buts Lonnie. Okay I'll tell you what, you leave that thing here and I'll pay for everything we do today." This time, he pulled out his phone then threw it on the sofa. My face lit up like he gave me a hand full of diamonds.

'*Maybe she's right, I have this wonderful woman. I know she loves me, and I can't give her a full day without letting my phone and the people on the other end come between us,*' Lonnie thought. Then he said, "You happy now?"

I answered with a soft kiss and a bright smile.

"See that's what I'm talking about. I sure hope you have plenty of money," added Lonnie.

"Don't worry", I said, "If I run out, I know where your pockets are." We both laughed and I gave him another soft kiss.

Since I was so adamant on paying for everything, Lonnie insisted that I drive too. We took the 45 minute ride to Ana Heim California. Over the next four hours, we did everything two people who are supposed to love each other could do at a fair. The rides, the games, we fed the animals, we held hands and my pretty smile was practically nonstop.

I almost forgot how much fun Lonnie could be. I hadn't enjoyed myself so much in years. But in the back of my mind, the one thing that I longed to hear him say today, he didn't. And now that I think about it, I should be upset. I've spent almost $200 and I can't even get him to say those three little words. "When Was The Last Time?" Throughout this warm beautiful day, he has done everything that says he loves me, but I wondered. "When Was the Last Time?" he actually said it aloud.

As a child my favorite thing about the fair was the Carrousel. With our caramel covered apples in hand I took Lonnie and led him over to the railing. Together we watched the children going around and round. The music and the sounds of their laughter took me back to when I was five or six. When Lonnie ran his fingers through my hair, it brought me back to the here and now. Then my first thought was, maybe he doesn't tell me what I long to hear because of the fact that I haven't been able to give him a child of his own. Knowing this, made me think again, "When Was the Last Time?"

"Lonnie, does it upset you that I haven't given you a son?"

"Hey, where did that come from?"

"I was just thinking about…" He didn't let me finish.

"No I'm not upset. Actually, it's nice having you all to myself. You share your beautiful body with me as much as I want. What do I have to be upset about?"

"Yeah, but a man should have a child."

"I understand, but when the time is right we'll have our first child. If not, before too much time goes by, we can always adopt one or two."

I never thought he would say such things. He said a lot in a very short time, but he didn't tell me he loves me. I know I should just ask him out right, but then I wouldn't like his answer because his yes will only be because I asked. He did call me beautiful, but that was only in reference to him sexing me. No! It's not the same.

"Hey, Lori, where did you go?"

"I was just thinking, When Was the Last Time?"

"What?" Lonnie asked.

"Nothing, what do you wanna do next?"

He answered by taking me into his arms and kissing me deeply. How can a woman be upset with a man that treats her like this? But even after a kiss like that, and the way he looked into my eyes, I still had to wonder, 'When Was the Last Time?'

"Come on, let's go home," Lonnie suggested.

I nodded my understanding and smiled up at him.

"Lonnie you know you have that look in your eyes."

"What look is that?"

"That look you get when you see me undressing for bed."

"I see you're very perceptive, 'cause when we get home that's just what I'm hoping you'll let me do, undress you and take you to bed."

All I could do was smile at him again. Then I took him by the hand and we headed for the exit. Along the way I grabbed one last cotton candy and fed most of it to this man I've loved for so many years. But why is it so hard for him to tell me he loves me? "Lonnie, would you really consider adopting a child?"

"Sure, why not? We have the means to support any kid and I know you would make the perfect mother. Why not adopt if we have to? You're a wonderful person; you've been beyond good to me, so yeah, why not?"

I felt so warm inside by his words. I asked Lonnie to drive us home, I wanted to sit back and just watch him. He has been so attentive to me all day, and the way he chose his words, there's just no way he doesn't love me, but, 'When Was the Last Time?' Before long we were home, and after we both took a quick shower, Lonnie made love to me deep into the night. Before closing his eyes and succumbing to sleep, he held me tightly and said, "Lori, you know I love you more than anything in this world, right?"

"Oh Lonnie I love you too. But baby please don't wait another two months to speak those words again."

When was the Last Time?

"That's how long it's been?"

"Yes, but it felt like a year." Once more he gave me those words I've longed to hear. Then he closed his eyes and slept until the sun came up. When I open my eyes the next morning, Lonnie was on his cell phone, and I wondered how long it will be until the next time?

While I Slept

The night was overly warm. It was well after mid-night and Erica, my wife, was fast asleep. She had been going through a lot in the last week and a half; we both have. Moving between work and taking care of our seven year old son, Turk, who was almost at the brink of death over some illness which no specialist could understand, Erica was at wits end. Then suddenly Turk was fine, fine as in never sick. Between the doctors and the two of us, we were all at a loss for an explanation.

To be honest, I wasn't as worried as to why he was back with us. He was fine, I had my boy back. Over the next couple of weeks I made a conscious decision to spend more time with Turk. We played more basketball in the driveway. He even took me for a walk in the park a few days ago. But ever since he became well again, there has been some kind of change around the house – around him even more so. I couldn't explain it, but I sure could feel it. It was one of those things that kept you up at night, like tonight. More than once I asked Erica if she noticed any changes in Turk, but she assured me everything was fine, our family could never be better. She was happy, and because of that, I was as well. But there was something wrong, I could feel it. Turk now had this intense look in his eyes. Although we spent much more time together, he barely spoke. We could have lunch, and he wouldn't eat. Erica said he was just being a kid, and I had no choice but to agree. Saturday evening Erica went to the store to get something for dinner. I told Turk to go get cleaned up before his mom came back. I sat down to watch the 5 o'clock news. I heard Turk go in to take a shower. I just sat back and tried to relax a bit. The house was quiet, but a few minutes later I heard a strange noise coming from Turk's room. I really thought nothing of it, but moments later I heard it again. I hit the mute on the remote control, and the only sound I could make out was the running of the shower.

Then I felt it, a chill. My mom used to say someone just walked over my grave whenever I got a chill on a warm day. But since I wasn't dead, I wanted to go into my room and grab my pistol. I got up and went to check on my son. As I turned into the hallway, I could clearly hear the shower. I went on to open the door to Turk's room and was greeted by a blast of cold air. "What the hell?" I thought, taking a step back. The rest of the house was nice and comfortable. We're in the middle of August and at 5 o'clock in the evening, it was still nice outside. I looked around the room. The window was open, but the room was almost freezing cold. I took one step inside and suddenly it felt like the rest of the house, normal.

"See, now I know you're trippin' Mike," I told myself. I looked around the room and it wasn't normal. The kid was seven years old and nothing was out of place. His bed was made; there were no clothes on the floor. None of his toys were thrown about. What the hell has he been in here doing? I was actually at a loss for words. I took a moment to walk around the room. Then I touched a few things and everything was as messy as the room of a seven-year-old usually was. My mind had to be playing tricks on me. Instead of worrying about Turk, I need to be worrying about me. Back on the couch I kicked my feet up, grabbed the remote and hit the mute button again.

The news reported another killing here in the city of Compton. When will Washington and it's so-called Politicians realize that the NRA is keeping the loop-holes open for way too many unnecessary weapons; and that they are ending up on the inner city streets? I closed my eyes and tried to get a little more comfortable. Erica should be back soon, I just hope she got something simple to make for dinner. Just as I was falling asleep, a blast of frigid air swept over my body. I sat up quickly, looked over my shoulder, and Turk was standing in the doorway. With a blank look on his face, he waved to me. "Hi dad, I'm done with my shower."

"Um, okay little man, go put some clean clothes on, and hopefully your mom will be back soon." For a long moment he just stood there and looked at me. Then he turned and walked to his room. I turned towards the TV, but had to look back at the doorway. I rubbed my arm knowing I felt the coldness. Where the hell was Erica? I shook off sleep and got up to go into the kitchen. I washed my hands and set out to make salad for dinner.

I was over the sink washing the lettuce, when I turned around to grab something; and Turk was standing right there in the doorway. Needless to say, he scared the hell out of me. He was so quiet, but not only that, I had only been in the kitchen for a few minutes – there was no way he could have gotten dressed that quickly. What was worst, his clothes were worn backwards except his shoes. How do you put on a button-up shirt backwards? Drying my hands I approached him, "What did you do boy, put your clothes on in the dark?" I had to make light of the situation, it was either that or think something most black people in this city don't think. Ghost, Bad Spirits, or some other Demonic shit.

But he just shrugged his shoulders. "Come here boy and let's fix your clothes before your mother comes home and thinks I've been in here abusing you. Turk come here." It took him a moment, but he entered the kitchen. As soon as I touched him, I thought I touched something no man should feel – an undead. I snatched my hand back and quickly stood up.

"What's wrong daddy?" He didn't ask like he was worried about me, but more like he wanted to eat me. I knew I was imagining things.

"Um, nothing"

I went to him once more, took hold of his shirt and pulled it over his head. This time he felt fine, but he was pale, if that's possible for a little Black kid. There were no marks or bruises on him. You know in movies, that is a telltale sign that somebody is about to get killed.

"Kick off your shoes" I told him as I put his shirt back on. I took his pants off and put them back on right. "Now put your shoes back on." Not wanting to think anything other than what it was – me needing a vacation, I went back to the sink and washed my hands again.

I looked around at Turk, he was doing as I asked, but this time he was putting his shoes on the wrong foot. "See now you're tripping boy. I don't know what's wrong with you, but you're seven and you know how to put your damn shoes on." He looked up at me with hurt in his eyes. I was on my way to saying something more when Erica walked in. Turk's face lit up like a light, he even fixed his shoes as they should be. Yes it had to be me. I gave Erica a kiss and went back to what I was doing.

"Hi baby", she said setting the bags down, "I see you started a salad?"

"Yeah, I thought I'd give you a hand. What did you buy?

"One of your favorites: Red Snapper, French Fries and white bread."

"That sounds good, I got plenty of hot sauce and I'm ready to eat."

"Mommy, mommy" Turk said, "Can I make the French Fries?"

"Sure honey, as long as you wash your hands, you can help."

"Mommy my hands are clean, daddy made me take a shower."

"Boy you sound like taking a shower is a chore," I told him. He laughed and wrapped his arms around his mother's waist.

In just under an hour the three of us had dinner on the table. Erica and Turk prayed over the food, while moments later I wished I had done the same. I bit into my fish and it was colder than the salad I made. I dropped the fork on the plate and it bounced onto the table cloth.

"Mike, what's wrong?" Erica asked.

"This fish…it's um…"

"What baby?"

I looked over at Turk and he almost had a smile on his face. "Is your food okay?" Erica asked.

"Yes, it's fine. As usual, you cooked a perfect dinner."

"Thank you baby"

"Thank you baby, thank baby you," Turk repeated several more times. Erica thought it was cute, but I thought there was nothing cute about it. In fact, it almost scared me. I took up my fork again and continued to eat. Then I realized the only thing that was cold was the Ketchup and Tartar sauce I put over my food. Dinner actually turned out nice, Turk was acting like his normal self again; he even made a bit of a mess. Erica and I talked about a little bit of everything, and I couldn't get enough of her smile. When we were done I cleared the table, while she made water to do the dishes.

Turk was sitting in the living room watching TV, so I made the two of us a bowl of ice cream and went to join him. He was watching an old rerun of the Giant Robot. He sat real close to me as we ate, it actually felt good having my baby boy enjoy being close to me. Before long Erica came to join us. Turk finished his ice cream and before I knew it he dozed off with his head in my lap. It was ten minutes past nine, and Erica kissed me good night. She took Turk and put him to bed. I spent another twenty or thirty minutes flipping through channels. When I couldn't find anything that I wanted to watch, I turned off the TV and went to make sure the house was locked up tightly.

Compton was still one of the most dangerous cities in the world, but little did I know, a few hours later I would have been safer out there, than in my own home. It was a quarter to twelve, Erica had been asleep for a few hours, but I was almost scared to close my eyes. Before she went to sleep I asked Erica about it, but she saw nothing wrong with the house or the people living in it. Another 45 minutes went by and just as I was drifting off, our bedroom door slowly creaked open. At first I thought I was seeing things, but when I cleared my eyes Turk was standing there covered in blood. I don't know where it came from, but I screamed louder than a five year old girl.

Erica jumped up in alarm. "Baby what's wrong? What's wrong?" All I could do was point at the door and the son I loved so much. "What?" Erica asked again. Turk was standing there with a large butcher knife in one hand and a dead chicken in the other.

"You can't see this shit?" I yelled. But before she could answer, Turk licked the chicken's bloody neck, then without warning he threw the butcher knife at us and it stuck in the head board just above our heads.

Once again Erica asked what was wrong with me, and again all I could do was point at Turk. He started chewing on the bloody neck of the chicken as I went hoarse screaming. Before going to bed I put my gun next to it and removed the safety. Erica reached over to sooth my face, but her hand went right through it. I tried to get out of bed, but it was like I was marred in mud. I reached for my gun, but it was frozen solid.

Turk and Erica began to laugh, and I screamed more and more, until I felt the prick on my arm. Moments later I heard a male voice saying I was coming out of it. Who in the hell was he, and what was I coming out of? I felt so hot and my throat burned like I swallowed a book of burning matches. I felt something grab my hand then I heard his voice. "Daddy please wake up." I was barely able to open my eyes, when I saw my amazing son. He smiled so bright it was like a wave of freshness washed over me. I was able to look around and I discovered where I was – in the hospital. I was hooked to everything in the room except the bathroom sink.

Then there was Erica, she touched my face, but her hand felt cold. A wave of fear washed over me, but when I opened my eyes again she smiled down on me, looking lovely as the day I married her. "What happened? How did I get here?"

"You were very sick baby."

"Yes Mr. Brown, West Nile Virus is very serious, for the last three weeks we have been pumping you full of IVs trying to bring your fever down. How do you feel?"

"Like Erica hit me with her car again."

"I've never done that."

"Okay", the doc said, "It sounds like you're out of the woods, we'll get some solid food into you and see how things will look tomorrow."

"Thank you so much Doctor" Erica said, "Thank you so much." He left and I swear the room became cold. Remembering most of what had to be a number of bad dreams, I shook it off. Erica and Turk looked fine, and happy to have me back. After another long two days, I was back at home. The weather later that morning was nice and clear for LA. Erica suggested I go get some rest and, without complaint, I went to do just that.

Everybody assured me I was fine, but when I opened our bedroom door, there was a butcher knife stuck in our headboard. Everything that I saw had to be a dream, just dreams. But then I got mad, somebody is crazy around here, and it ain't me. To prove my theory, or theirs, I slowly walked over to the headboard. I reached for the knife; it was solid to the touch. I pulled it from the head board and went to find my so called family. I'm not crazy I said several times from the bedroom to the kitchen. Erica and Turk were in there, about to have lunch. For a long moment I stood still and watched them. These were not just dreams I told myself, something wasn't right. This knife was real; it was a living fact to that. Turk was trying to kill me, and Erica was telling him to do it, I could feel it.

I gripped the knife several times in my hand. I must protect myself I thought. But why are they trying to kill me? I asked myself again. But before I could give myself time to answer, I walked over and brought the knife down into the back of Erica's neck. Without taking it out, I slammed her against the wall. I looked over at Turk and all I saw was his seven year old smile, but it was still dark and evil. I pulled the knife from her neck, and before she could slide to the floor I stabbed her several more times. Turk got up from the table and clapped his hands. The knife slung blood all over the kitchen, even on to the boy. He licked at some of the blood and clapped his hands again. "She tastes good daddy."

His words made me take a step back; then Turk dropped to his knees and began playing in his mother's blood. He put his hand prints everywhere, the stove, the floor, the wall, and even himself. My head screamed at me to do something; that I need to kill him as well. I listened to my thoughts, I plunged the knife into Turk's little body several times just so the screaming would stop. But he never yelled or cried out; there was just this look in his eyes.

Not totally understanding why, but when he closed his eyes in death, I was able to stop my arm. The realization of what I just did suddenly came to me. Not knowing why there was blood everywhere, or why a large knife was in my hand, I threw the knife into the sink and turned out the light, but there was another light floating above them. It wasn't bright but I could see it all the same. I'd never seen anything like it except in books, and so I ran from the house and out into the street fearing the worse that might happen. The day was silent all around me, all except this beeping sound.

It was almost unbearable to my ears, yet I couldn't open my eyes to see where it was coming from. But the beeping was raising forth a scream within me; then it was gone. "Mr. Brown can you hear me?" I opened my eyes but all I saw was orange, then I realized I hadn't opened my eyes at all; the bright sun from the window was shining on my face. This time when I heard my name my eyes did open. "Nice to have you back Mr. Brown. I'm Doctor Cruz. You have been in the hospital for over a month. I'll have a nurse call your wife; I know she's dying to see that you're awake." It took a lot, but I was able to grasp his arm and shook my head no.

"They're dead, I killed them," I said closing my eyes.

"No Mr. Brown, they're fine, they have been here almost daily."

"Please Doc, I need some time alone, I know I ki…"

"I understand. I'll get someone to bring you something to eat, and I'll come back and check on you a little later."

"Hey Doc" Before he left the room I asked why I was here.

"You contracted West Nile Virus."

"Are you sure that's what it was? Because I'm almost positive I…I…"

"Mr. Brown that's what all the test results show. You're fine, and your family's fine." He left the room, and for once I felt good. I turned to look out the window, it was so nice outside. When the nurse comes to check on me, I'll ask her to call Erica. I sat up in bed to get more comfortable, and a moment later the nurse came in.

After blinking my eyes a few times, I screamed. She was covered in blood. I closed my eyes tightly, not knowing whether I was still asleep, dead or alive, but I vowed never to open them again.

Coming Home

"James you feel that?"

"What an earth quake?"

"No you old fool. It feels like something is coming."

"Emma you know I love you, but you need to stop drinking that old pickle juice."

"I'm telling you James, something good is coming."

"Well it sure ain't in all these bills that are here on this table."

"Don't worry James, we've come across hard times before and we've made it through."

"Yeah I know, but not like this. The Government has taken half my check, and no matter how much I call, no one can tell me why."

"You know James Jr. said we could use the money he sent home."

"Emma that boy is off fighting at war, there's no way I'm gonna use his savings. Besides, that $3,000 isn't gonna help nobody. And the $50 you're sending to that other boy in prison every month ain't helping him or us."

"James that boy is your son."

"Woman I'd rather eat this $200 light bill than call him my son."

"James please don't talk like that. What I wish you would do, is pray for them both to come home." While James sat at the table opening more bills in disdain, I went to wipe down the kitchen counters. Moments later the doorbell rang. James got up slowly from the table to go answer it.

"Oh my god, my god! Emma come quick!" He yelled to me. When I came from the kitchen, James had James Jr. in a big hug. Then my baby came to embrace me, almost picking me up off the floor.

"James didn't I tell you? Didn't I tell you? Thank you Jesus, you brought my baby home. Come on in here. Are you hungry? Let me make you something to eat."

On the way back into the kitchen, James Jr. dropped his bag by the couch and took off his uniform jacket. "I can't believe my boy has finally come home. How long are you home for?"

"For good pop. My tour of duty is over."

"Are you going to re-enlist?"

"I don't know mom, right now I just wanna enjoy some of your fine cooking." His words dearly touched my heart. As I was rummaging around for something to cook, the doorbell rang once more. "You two talk, I'll go get it." Moments later I screamed, and they both came running from the kitchen to find me hugging Kevin.

"Who is it Emma?"

"Look who's here James." But he was less than enthused.

"Ah baby brother, how in the hell did you get out of prison?"

"He probably broke out" James said sarcastically.

"Hi pop, nice to see you too," Kevin said.

"Oh my god James, they're here, both of my babies are home, safe and sound."

"Well I bet this one won't be here long."

"James don't talk like that."

"It's okay mom, I know he missed me," said Kevin.

"Yeah about as much as I'd miss having Colon Cancer." Even though it hurt to hear his dad speak of him like that, Kevin still managed to laugh with his brother.

"Come on here baby, I was just making your brother something to eat."

"Good, I need some real food; I didn't have anything on the way home. I've been waiting on this for a long time mom," Kevin said.

"Boy I thought you didn't like yo mama's cooking the way you keep running off to that prison," James Sr. said sarcastically.

"Don't worry pop," James Jr. said, "I'll keep him out this time."

"I don't know how you plan to do that, them folks was able to raise him more than I was."

"Well you don't have to worry about that any more pop, James and I have been talking over the last few years, and we have a plan," said Kevin.

While I was washing off some vegetables to make a salad I asked, "What kind of plan have you been talking about baby?"

"We are gonna try and go into business for ourselves."

"That sounds good baby, you guys can do anything if you pray about it."

"Well iffin' you do start a business, you best be puttin' it next to Folsom State Prison, so that boy," James said pointing to Kevin, "won't have to go far once he steals you blind."

"I just can't do nothing right when it comes to you, can I pop?" Kevin replied.

"Boy you could read and write your name by the time you was three, so that let me and yo mama know you was special. But somewhere down the road you decided you'd rather pick up somebody else's money over a book. It caused you to spend most of your life behind bars. I'm just glad you didn't bring James down with you."

"Pop, James ain't no angel either!"

"Boy compared to you, that boy is like the Second Coming." Kevin just shook his head. "Now what kind of business y'all plan on starting?" James Sr. asked.

"We haven't quite figured that out yet pop, but Kevin thinks we should start an auto parts store."

"Son, they got them thangs on every corner"

"Well I like it," I told them.

"And where is y'all gonna get the money to start this? Boy you didn't rob somebody on the way here, did you?"

"Pop will you lay off him? He wants this as much as I do. Besides, I have a little money saved and I can get a VA loan."

"Son you got $3,000 saved, and you lucky I was able to talk your mama out of paying down some of these high ass bills."

"James watch your mouth in this house," I told him.

"Everyone is broke, even the government, let them tell it."

"Don't worry pop, we'll figure out something, you'll see," James Jr. replied.

An hour after dinner, James Jr. and Kevin took my car and left the house. "So where are we headed little bro?"

"Nowhere in this hood. I've been gone five years, and only one or two of these fools ever thought about me. Jump on the freeway and head out to Anaheim. I wanna show you something," Kevin answered.

"What's up?" James Jr. said, giving Kevin a look.

"While I was on the inside, one of my boys heard me talking to you about starting this business. He heard how we didn't have much startup money, so he put me up on some game."

"What's that?"

"You'll see." Another fifteen minutes had passed, and Kevin told James Jr where to get off the freeway. It was 10:35 pm and Anaheim was quiet. They found the address that Kevin read off a strip of paper. "What's up?" James Jr. asked for the second time.

"That right over there," He said pointing at a strip mall and a jewelry store that sat in the middle of it.

"Fool, what you pointing at that for? We are not about to rob that store. I told you I'm going to takeout a couple of loans and we'll be alright."

"But what if they don't give you the money? I don't wanna be out here in these streets James, because I know I'm gonna screw up and go back to the pen."

"What do you think is going happen if you rob that store?"

"I told you bro, I have all the game on this place. The boy's auntie owns it, and he once worked there. He wants someone to take the place now because she wouldn't hire him a lawyer."

"Come on Kevin, I'm a U.S. soldier, I can't be out here robbing jewelry stores."

"I feel you bro, but I wanna open this store as much as you do, I just don't know of any other way to get the money we'll need."

"Don't worry little bro, I got you. We won't have to do this, you'll see." He gave Kevin some dap and they headed back home.

The next morning James Jr. rose early and started making calls. Those calls lasted into the afternoon, but no one was willing to take a chance without any collateral. Frustrated, James Jr. went down to the kitchen for a snack. Mom and pop were there. "What's wrong son?" You look like you got drafted again."

"Nah pop, I've been on the phone all the day trying to secure a loan for our business, and no one wants to loan me any money."

"Son didn't I tell you this whole country is in a bad way?"

"Yes, but pop there has to be a bank out there willing to take a chance on us."

"Boy you'd have better luck raising that kind of money with me giving you $20, and you going out and finding a dice game."

"James! You can't tell him things like that," I interjected.

"Well it's true woman."

"Baby, mama told you to pray on it, and I'm sure something will come about," I advised sincerely.

"I will mom." He got up, took an apple and went back to his room.

James Jr. was on his computer still searching when Kevin came in. "What's up little bro?"

"What's up with you? You don't look so good."

"I'm not, I tried all day to get someone to loan us the money we would need, but I was unsuccessful."

"What are we going to do?"

"I don't know, but we are not going to that store again." In a week, James Jr. had barely stepped foot out of the house, and there was just no money out there; even the VA Loan would take anywhere from one to two years they said. Then Kevin told James Jr. how easy taking the jewelry store would be. "But we don't have any guns." Without a second thought, he pulled out one from under his shirt.

"You was sayin'."

Once again James Jr. gave Kevin that look, but he turned his back on Jr. He let it go and went and threw himself across the bed. James Jr. shook his head and told himself over and over again they can't do that shit, but two hours later they were parked not far from the store. James didn't want to talk because he was sure he would change his mind. By 7:00 pm he found himself where he never thought he would be. But within minutes they had a bag full of jewelry and money and were on thier way back home. But a block before they reached the freeway James Jr. ran across a police car. Somehow the cop just knew they were bad guys and hit his lights. By the time the police turned around, the brothers made it around the next corner, James Jr. stopped and made Kevin take the bag and get out.

The next morning I was up early to receive the mail, and got so excited. "James, James come quick! I don't believe it, I knew if we prayed hard enough the Lord would answer."

"Emma, what you going on about?"

"It's for you, the Government has sent you your back pay."

"Let me see that."

Coming Home

"Hot damn Emma, there's a check for $15,000 in here. Emma this is enough to pay off the bills and we can give the rest to the boys. And if there's a little left, we can buy you a stripper pole for our bedroom."

"James sir, you know I'm too old for that sort of thing."

"Emma, you're only as old as you feel, now come give me some sugar." I wiped my hands on my apron, smiling I came over to the table and put my arms around the man I've loved for over forty years. "Now where are them boys? I wanna surprise them."

Moments later while James reread his letter, I went to the door and called for the boys. Kevin came in looking haggard. "What's up mom?"

"Boy what's wrong with you?" James asked, "Did you sleep out there with the dog? Where's your brother?"

"I don't know pop."

"Well, look here, me and your mom want you guys to have this." He handed Kevin the check, and upon seeing $15,000 Kevin almost started to cry. "Boy what's wrong with you?"

"Nothing!" He ran from the room.

Over the next two days we waited for James Jr. to come home, but after the first day Kevin knew he wasn't coming. I was beside myself. Pop knew something was very wrong and took it out on Kevin. By 9:00am the following morning the doorbell rang. The three of us came from different parts of the house to see who it was. I answered the door and when the Detective spoke his first words, I broke out in tears. Kevin wanted to break out the back of the house, and pop tried to push him into the arms of the Detective.

Kevin got his brother killed. Everyone seemed to be able to feel his guilt, but Kevin's lies seem to convince them otherwise – that he wasn't involved, for now.

That night, in Kevin's dreams, his mom's words would haunt him. "My baby will never come home again." And a few months later Kevin wondered if she would say the same about him. Since James Jr. was dead, pop's had no good reason to give Kevin any parts of the $15,000. So running low on the money they stole, he finally decided to go out and try to sell the jewelry. But he made an illegal right turn and was stopped by the police. Everything was in order as far as paper work, so Kevin didn't try to run. But since he was on parole, the cop pulled Kevin out to search the car. The only thing left to say is, he never came home again either.

When was the Last Time? Part 2

Three days had passed. Then a week, and before I knew it, two more weeks went by; Lonnie had been working like crazy at his law firm. I know he wants nothing more than to take care of me and to make sure I have everything I need, but when was the last time? I have been holding this feeling inside, trying not to say anything. But the news I found out a few days ago is really making it harder and harder to say nothing. I was standing in the window of our loft, looking down on the sun lit street. There were very few people moving about, but I stayed there with my hand over my stomach. The warm sun coming through the window felt so good on my skin, but I had so many mix emotions, I honestly didn't know which way to turn.

Lonnie promised he would not let long periods of time go by without saying he loved me, but when was the last time? Looking down I said, "I hope you will be able to keep him home a little more often." It was Saturday and he should be home, but I told myself, "You know what? He's out there trying to provide for me." So before turning away from the window and its warmth I told myself everything is fine with us. And I'm going to have a surprise waiting for him when he comes home. I put a big smile on my face thinking about the man I love, and went out shopping. A couple of hours later, I was back. When Lonnie came home from work, I had the whole house smelling like Chinese food. Egg rolls, Sweet and Sour Pork, Wong-Ton Soup, and a fresh salad. There was a bottle of white wine chilling in a bucket of ice, and soft music playing in the background.

When Lonnie came in, he was tied to his cell phone. After he dropped his coat and brief case on the chair by the door and continued to talk, I got annoyed. Walking over to him I said, "Hang up." He looked at me. "Hang up Lonnie," I repeated.

"Um, Mr. Wright I understand your position fully, but we're gonna have to continue this on Monday when I get back to my office." They exchanged pleasantries and he hung up the phone. I guess the smells and the music got his attention and he took me in his arms. "It smells wonderful in here. You did all this for me?"

"Why wouldn't I? I love you." I thought for sure he would return the sentiment, but he kissed me instead. I loved it, but I couldn't help but wonder; when was the last time?

When we broke our embrace, I led him to the table. "Are you hungry?"

"Are you beautiful?" His words made me touch my stomach. I smiled and poured him a glass of wine. He didn't notice that I didn't have any. But when was the last time? Why is it so hard for him to say he loves me?

"Did you have a hard day at work?"

"Not really. Actually I made twenty thousand dollars today."

"That's nice, and you know how much you love money."

"Lori, know you didn't. You spend money twice as fast as I do. Look at this place." He said gesturing around the loft. When he laughed I blushed, bent down and kissed him. I made our plates and he ate two helpings. "Lori I loved that meal." Yeah I thought, but what about me?

"I'm glad you enjoyed it. Can I get you anything else?"

"Um yeah" And I could see that look in his eyes; he wanted our bodies to be close. He's not lacking in that department, but when was the last time? When was the last time he told me he loves me? When he rose I got up as well. We went into the living room with his wine. He sat on the couch and pulled me into his lap. "Lori, are you okay?" I was caught off guard with that one. I looked deep into his eyes and willed him to see inside of me. I can tell him a thousand times I love him, but it seem so hard for him to do the same. Then I wondered if my mother went through this.

"Yes, it's nothing that being in your arms can't fix." He kissed me deeply and I could feel his heartbeat, and not to mention another part of him.

"Lori there's something I need to tell you." Here it comes; finally he is gonna say it. But the words he spoke almost made me say the hell with "I love you." "I've been thinking a lot about something we talked about when we went to the fair." I had to think about it, and then it hit me.

"Oh Lonnie, please tell me you're talking about what I think you're talking about?"

"If you're thinking about adopting a baby, then yeah." I hugged him so tight; then I jumped up.

"Are you serious?"

"Yes! Actually I made some calls the other day, and I think I found us a beautiful baby girl we can adopt."

"Oh Lonnie I love you so much. When can we go see her?"

"We have an appointment this coming Tuesday. Is that okay with you?"

"Yes, yes, I can't wait." Then I thought about my own secret I've been holding onto for the last week, and I touched my stomach. But will he still wanna go through with it if he knows I'm pregnant? "Lonnie when was the last …?" Lonnie do you…? Look Lonnie, no matter what I'm about to tell you, promise me you won't change your mind about adopting a baby."

"What is it?"

"Just promise me." He looked at me for a long moment, then he agreed.

I rubbed my stomach and I guess the gesture registered in his head. "Lori, are you saying what I think you're saying?"

"If you're thinking I'm saying I'm having a baby, then yeah, that's what I'm saying." He jumped to his feet, picked me up and spun us around. I could see the joy on his face, but when was the last time? Moments later I had my answer, because he laid me on the couch and started removing my clothes. With every kiss he said "I…love…you" When we were done making love he put his head to my stomach and said,

"I love you both." Several times he repeated it. The gesture brought tears to my eyes.

"Lonnie, promise me something."

"Anything my love"

"Promise you'll say that more, and promise we can have more babies."

"I love you beyond words, and you can have as many rug rats running around here as you can stand." We both laughed, then my kiss told him to make love to me again."

The Shit Didn't Work

"Good morning ladies and gentleman. My name is Dr. Max Foresight. You have all agreed to be here today, to take part in a medical trial to determine if people can actually remember dreams from start to finish. Often times when we dream, we only remember small portions of them. But before we go any further, would the ten of you please write down your cell phone numbers here on this pad".

"Make sure you include your names." I gave them a moment. "Now let's begin. Over the years here at the Behavior Unit of Unique Technologies, we have been trying to develop clear and concise ways to read and interpret dreams. People have dreams almost nightly, more often than not, those dreams are not just random, they have important meaning, not only to those dreaming them, but we believe to the world."

"It is our hope that the ten of you, through our new technology called 'Simplify', will be able to help us interpret those dreams, from start to finish."

"Doc, when you say 'Technology,' exactly what are you referring to?" I flipped through my chart of names and photos.

"You're Lacy Brighten correct?"

"Yes Doctor."

"Well Ms. Brighten, we have developed dissolvable nanos that each of you will take, and this nano will record each of your dreams over a two week period." That couldn't have been any further from the truth. "At the conclusion of the two weeks, the nano will disintegrate and pass out of the body through normal bodily functions."

"You mean to tell us, you're going to implant a bunch of robots in our heads so you can see what we're thinking?" "Did this yahoo hear me say anything about implanting something inside of them?"

"Um, no Mr." I flipped through my files again. "No Mr. Smalls, it's nothing like that. We are not implanting anything, you will swallow a pill and it shall be painless."

"I don't know," said Mr. Smalls, "this sounds dangerous."

"I assure you, it's perfectly safe." But little did they know what I actually had in mind for them would be more dangerous than anything any of them have ever done before; except for one perhaps. "Are there any more questions?"

"Yes, my name is York, Steven York."

"Yes Mr. York."

"We were told that for these experiments we would be paid $5,000, is that true?"

"Yes, that is correct." But little did they know that I would make a few million from the ten of them.

Because of my gambling addiction and my wife's taste in expensive clothes and jewelry, I had racked up almost $200,000 in debt. So I was going to use these seven women and three men to get out of debt. "Okay ladies and gentlemen let's begin." I picked up a remote control, and pressed one button to call for my assistant. "Ladies and gentleman this is Shelly." She came in carrying a tray of ten small plastic see-through cups. Each contained one sugar tablet, nothing more. In essence a placebo. "Please do not chew these, they will dissolve on their own." Shelly passed them out, some members of the group were a little hesitant, but they did as I asked.

"Hey these are good." Lucy Brighten said.

"Yes," I responded looking at my watch, "and they should be just about gone." Everyone was all smiles so I dismissed Shelly. Once Shelly exited the room I pushed another button on the remote. Moments later the lights in the room dimmed. Three large monitors came on showing flames. With yet another push of a button I was able to recline their chairs.

"Hey Doc," the only African American in the room said, "This is cool, what's next: strippers?" Everyone laughed. His name was Cotton Blake, and I could tell, out of everyone else, he would work out the best. At twenty nine, he owns a Sports Bar in Huntington Beach, Calif. Fit as any track star, and smart as any Harvard student. But in my eyes, I desired to have him here the most because as a juvenile he was busted for burglarizing three Home Depots stores. All three were done in the same night!

Cotton and one other guy would enter the buildings. While Cotton would cut open the safes, his partner scouted for other valuables. After the heist, Cotton had close to $90,000 in his mother's home. However, his partner got nabbed while out selling a dozen laptop computers. With the first mention of prison time, he divulged where the authorities could find Cotton. Cotton spoke very little, and just did his time. Now it was my hope that he would complete the mission I assign him like he did as a juvenile.

Over the next twenty minutes I talked to them as they watched the flames. Although they could not readily see it, the flames were telling the group to listen to my words; that they were to do as I commanded them. They were being brainwashed to follow the commands issued when I call them on their cell phones. The phrase, 'the flames are on,' would prompt them to ask what their mission is and follow my orders. "Ms. Brighten, can you hear me?" She didn't speak, she just nodded her head yes. "Good, now I want you to get up and walk around the room backwards." As I knew she would, she got up and did as I asked.

No one else in the room paid her any attention. When she came back to her seat, I asked her to sit back down. "Remember, the flames are your guide, when you hear that the flames are on, you will do as I ask."

"Yes Doctor," the group said as one. Using the remote control I lowered the flames from the monitors while repeating that the flames were their guide. Just before the last of the flames were gone from the monitors, there was a loud horn that blared somewhere just outside the building. I thought nothing of it, but I did see several in the group blink their eyes.

I snapped my fingers in a subtle way, not loud, but it got their attention. "Ladies and gentleman remember, our dreams are what drive us, they are not to be ignored. Your dreams can tell us so much, it is up to you to listen. How do you guys feel?"

"I feel hungry." Cotton said.

"Okay folks, by now the nanos have worked their way into your Cerebral Cortex. As you can see, none of you have had any bad reactions, so tonight, if and when you dream, nothing will change. I assure you you're safe. Now if you give me a moment I will have Shelly bring in some lunch."

"That's what I'm talkin' about," Cotton said.

Beforehand I had studied the ten of them. I knew those who were gun owners, and those who were not. I knew what possible targets were close to their homes. Now it was time to set them out to work.

The first week went by smoothly, there were reports of several bank robberies, and two local jewelry stores were also robbed. Each of the ten completed their first mission. I had them all meet me in different parts of the city. Cotton came in with over $300,000, but to my surprise, during our meeting he called me by my name. I worried some but, he didn't question me on why we were together.

The second week passed, I didn't quite make the two million I was after, but was more than close. So, Friday morning I called for the ten of them to come in. The office was somewhat quiet, so no one questioned why they were there. I had them all seated, lowered the lights, and turned on the monitors. The flames came on and I began to talk them down. For the first time I noticed how they were all agitated.

"Relax everyone, just relax," I told them. There was a phone that rang outside the office that no one answered. Cotton and the others were very restless. I continued to talk them down. Then from outside there was a loud blare of a horn, and without warning the ten of them open their eyes. I called Lucy Brighten by name, but she didn't answer. I called Cotton, he as well didn't answer. But they all advanced towards me. I moved towards the door, but someone grabbed me by my lab coat.

"The flames are your guide," I yelled to them. Before I could repeat my words, the ten of them were ripping at my clothes, tearing them from my body. I yelled with everything I had, yet no one came from the outside. The group began to consume my body whole. I still tried to yell that the flames were their guide. My last thoughts were, "How did I turn a group of thieves into a group of man eaters?"

Excerpt from "Fight to Breathe" the Shannon Briggs story by Rahsaan Thomas

Prologue

I was conceived fighting for my very existence. My mother was said to have been barren, unable to grow life in her womb. She didn't want kids anyways. So it was a shock and unwanted surprise when she got pregnant. I was born an undesired preemie, three months early. During the first few days of my birth, it wasn't clear if I would live or have a mother if I did.

Things changed once a nurse convinced Margie Parham to at least take a look at me. She didn't want to. She came to New York City with stars in her eyes, hoping to live the lavish life. Having a child would cramp her style and hamper her plans. Then she took one look at me and love flooded her heart. Thereafter, she never wanted to put me down.

I survived premature birth too. It wasn't easy, nor did I make it unscathed. One year later I came home from the hospital with the chronic condition--asthma. To this day, sometimes it's a fight just to keep air in my lungs.

My next biggest battle was for survival. Mom doted on her only child and life was good until 1985. We were upper poor class, but I didn't know it. With her RN salary, mom had us living in Atlantic Towers, an apartment complex that resembled luxury condos. The fact they were located in the notorious Brownsville section of Brooklyn escaped me. There was always food on our table, designer clothes on my back and all the toys I could want. Plus I went to a private school. We seemed rich compared to those around me. Then poverty ambushed me.

The pillars that held up my world fell down on top of me. My father committed a crime and went into hiding. America's most wanted numbered his days on the run. Then mom lost control to heroin addiction. I came home to find our locks missing, furniture gone and yellow tape forming an X across the doorway, like it was a crime not to pay your rent. I didn't know what was going on until seeing an eviction notice taped there. The murmurs of neighbors, who seemed happy for our demise, further clarified things. We were thrown out for past due rent.

I ended up homeless once heroin took my mother past the point of no return. No family member was willing to take me in. Through sleeping in a boxing gym, I discovered a way to survive--the ring. Boxing became my way of life.

The thing about boxing though, is that most of the bouts take place outside the ring. Twisted contracts, grimy managers, disloyal fans, battles with PTSD; expectations of others, media images, the deaths of both my parents and my own anger.

Despite it all, I became heavy weight champion two times. This is the story of my life, a fight to breathe.

Excerpt from the soon-to-be-released memoir "From Guns to God" by Rahsaan Thomas

Those who don't understand their history are doomed to make the same mistakes in the future. It was my history that made me who I am and predetermined that I would kill in the situation I got myself into. To better understand, I need to go back to the beginning...

SECTION 1: GUNS

CHAPTER 1

"WE WERE ALL IN THE HOOD AS BEGINNERS, BUT SOMETHING MUST HAVE GOT IN US, BECAUSE WE ALL TURNED INTO SINNERS." –AZ

I was born Rahsaan Sanchez on September 22, 1970 in Kings County Hospital, Brooklyn, New York. My mother was from Farragut projects, by downtown Brooklyn. However, when I was six, she moved my two year old brother Hakeem and I to the Brownsville section of Brooklyn, in 1976.

Brownsville used to be a Jewish and Italian neighborhood. By the time we moved in, all the Jews and Italians were replaced by Blacks and Puerto Ricans. Many of the former residents still kept businesses in the area, especially on Pitkin and Belmont Avenues. There, stores like Harry's; Simon's clothing and sneakers; along with the pizza shop and furniture stores sold their items at reasonable prices often with no tax to the now almost exclusively Black and Hispanic neighborhood.

Hakeem and I were first left with my aunt in Van Dyke projects in the heart of Brownsville until our apartment on Rockaway Avenue was ready. Sheila, my mother's elder sister, babysat us for about a month along with her own kids, Angel and Deangelo. Both were older than me by 3 and 2 years respectively. We were close like sister and brothers, although they often raked on me. Their favorite running joke was singing, "PLAY THE FUNKY MUSIC WHITE BOY," because of my extremely light complexion.

Just a few blocks away, at 10 Amboy in Marcus Gravey Village, lived a bunch of my cousins off and on. Dee Dee, Man and Arlyn sometimes stayed there with our great aunt Dee.

Once our apartment was ready, we moved into Atlantic Towers at 216 Rockaway Avenue between Atlantic and Pacific streets. The towers had two 24 story buildings with about 17 apartments on each floor that had terraces. From the top of the buildings, you could see all of Brownsville and beyond. Between the buildings were two full basketball courts, a barbecue pit, slide and swing sets and a swimming pool, as if the Towers were a luxury condo development. Maybe it could have been just that if there weren't at least 10 different housing projects nearby in the small community.

I can't say I was living in an almost all Black ghetto filled with housing projects that corrupted me. I remember how my mother and two other single moms left their doors unlocked all day. We all lived on the second floor and would go back and forth between each other's pads at will. The doors stayed unlocked until the 1980s, when crack hit the hood hard.

I can't blame the lack of a father because my mother is a super-woman. She is the definition of perseverance, determination and no excuses. Somehow, without any major help, she worked full time, graduated from college with a bachelor's degree in sociology and raised my brother and me without a man or compromise.

No matter how bad things looked, she remained honest. One time she found a wallet with over $100 in it. Not only did she return the wallet, but she also left the money inside even though there was an eviction notice on our door for the past due rent. She did what she had to do, but always stayed within moral and legal bounds. In fact, she worked 60-80 hours a week as long as I can remember. First by working two jobs, then as a correctional officer for New York City's Department of Corrections on Riker's Island doing double shifts. She is truly a woman of character.

She sacrificed her own goals, hopes and dreams to make sure we made something of ourselves. Her heart was in baking cakes in shapes and designs of characters and objects. She is so good at it that investors and clients alike lined up to help her open a bakery.

However, with two kids, she wouldn't take the gamble of giving up medical benefits and a definite pay check to be an entrepreneur.

She also gave up her spare time to prepare us for a better life. She had Hakeem and I taking art and computer classes at Brooklyn College before we entered high school. She took us to our little league baseball games and she was the den mother of our Boy Scout troop. Plus she bust her butt to keep us in private schools. My mother did more for us by herself than most two parents do.

Even still, the murder of my father did have some effect. We weren't close. I don't remember anything about him prior to when that man started coming around in 1982. All of a sudden, this missing person was coming to pick me up for the weekends. Moms hated him with a passion for some unexplained reason and put Carlos through hell to see us; meaning, if he wanted to see me, my brother who wasn't his son had to come too. If he wanted to buy me anything, Hakeem had to receive the same thing. Plus he wasn't allowed in our apartment. Carlos had to ring the intercom, get cursed out and wait downstairs. I was touched that a stranger would go through so much trouble to see me.

I tried to front -- like him coming around meant nothing. After all, he was gone by my second birthday. Moms remarried Hakeem's pops, but he was gone by the time I turned four. I was used to not having a male figure around except for our uncle Boo Boo. However, when Carlos asked me to be the ring boy at his wedding to another woman, I was hurt. The only outward sign though was the "accidental" dropping of the ring on the way down the aisle. When he had my little brother, Carlos Sanchez III, by the other lady, I felt jealous too. I think we all have an emotional bond with the people whose DNA we carry.

One day Carlos stopped coming around. Nobody said anything and I never asked after him. I figured it was just too much trouble to afford his new wife, her daughter, my new brother, Hakeem and I. Plus, with all the verbal abuse mom launched at him, I could hardly blame him.

His parents, Grandma Jenny and Grandpa Carlos Sanchez Senior, always picked up the slack. I saw them regularly even after they retired from janitor jobs at Bishop Loughlin High School and moved from Brooklyn to Puerto Rico. I even spent two summers in Santa Isabella with them.

Then one day, grandma told me why Carlos II "disappeared." He was found in the back of a bar with his throat cut and wallet missing. She took months to break the news in order to spare my feelings, but I took it calmly.

I didn't cry or anything, but for some reason, I never spoke to my Puerto Rican grandparents again. I never kept in touch with my little brother Carlos. It was like when news of pops death reached me, his side of the family died with him. I can't put my finger on any outward effect losing my father had, but something changed in me afterwards. Like the crack epidemic, Dad's death didn't have a direct affect, but it was a cumulative factor.

Moms sought to have my last name changed to Thomas (her maiden name) once he died. She had wanted it changed for years, feeling he deserved no credit because she raised me without him. I liked the name Sanchez better because it represented my Puerto Rican side, but she did have a point. He wouldn't give her the necessary permission for the name change while alive, however, Carlos's untimely departure from this world cleared the way. By the time I was 18, the paperwork went through and my last name became Thomas.

Drugs affected our household from outside in. My mother didn't use drugs and neither did I. Determined not to be like her alcoholic mother, she never drank liquor. However, the crack epidemic did hit Brownsville hard in the mid-1980s and that's around the time my troubles went to a whole new level.

My single biggest problem was how I looked. Pops was a tall, handsome Puerto Rican with a medium built and a big curly afro. My mother is a beautiful light skin sister. Somehow, I came out looking like my mother, with my father's hair texture and the complexion of a White person. If not for the size of my lips, nose and the texture of my hair, there would be no clues that I wasn't White. Plus, I was tall, lanky, with a pretty boy face and the athleticism of a nerd. In other words, I looked like prey and the reason for our opposition in the hard streets of Brownsville.

In addition to natural looks, my school uniform was like a bull's eye to bullies. From 1st to 8th grades, I attended Our Lady Loretto

Catholic School. It was mandatory that we wore blue pants, a white button down shirt and a blue and grey plaid tie. For some reason, public school kids sought to beat up Catholic school ones.

I was hated on sight beyond reason. Standing out like a fluorescent light in the dark made me the object of oppression. The White man generally got the blame for all the problems tickled down on us by that unseen hand. They called me, "White boy!", "Cracker" and claimed I thought I was better than them. Who ever read my mind and started that rumor got it wrong because I thought of no such thing. I tried to explain that "I'M NOT EVEN WHITE, I'M HALF BLACK AND PUERTO RICAN," but nobody cared. I looked White and White people, including look-a-likes, were disliked in my hood.

Somebody was always messing with me. It started out with public school kids cutting class to come up to Our Lady of Loretto looking to start trouble. When the pugnacious youths came around, mostly everybody cleared out. However, since I couldn't run very fast, I didn't even try. When they picked a fight with me, I stood my ground and defended myself, win or lose.

My best friend at Loretto, William Boyland, didn't have any problems. His pops was the Brownsville assembly man, Thomas Boyland, who Hopkinson Avenue was renamed in honor of. Will must have learned the gift of gab from his dad, because he was able to talk his way out of drama. He is probably the only friend whose father stayed around that I've ever had. Maybe that's the difference a father makes because while Will never fought, I had to fight constantly. I was the underdog, who lacked people skills but had the heart of a lion.

The problems weren't only at school. Dudes from the Towers stayed on me also. An older dude we called Daddy O was the main one who called me "WHITEBOY" with malice in his voice and instigated those my age to fight me. Plus he judged many bouts I felt I won as losses on my hood score card. Evidence of bloodied noses, busted lips and black eyes blended into the dark complexions of my opponents and disappeared once they cleaned up. Meanwhile, my light skin highlighted all wounds, therefore people believed him. Come what may, I refused to follow him or except "Whiteboy" as a handle, so I stayed a loner and kept fighting.

Back in the 70s, I mostly got fair fights. When someone did jump me, an adult passing by would break up the bouts. Plus since I didn't know how to fight, I lost many of the early ones, so there was no need to jump me.

In the early-mid 80s things changed. With over 100 fights lending experience as my teacher, I started winning most of the battles and that's when it became more likely I would get jumped. Also, adults became less likely to break up fights because, as teenagers, we were bigger and meaner. Meanwhile, my little brother, four years younger was useless. He would just stand there and cry while I fought, even during the ones I won.

On one occasion, I was winning a fight against Commando, a kid my age I didn't get along with, when his little brother, Dayday jumped in. It started as a one on one, but as he was losing, Daddy O whispered something to Day. Next thing I know, Day leaped onto my back, giving Commando a chance to hit me a couple of times. Then the large crowd started yelling "UH-OH," as Hakeem could be seen approaching. With him being the same age as Dayday, the bout shaped up to be a battle of the brothers. However, Hakeem got beat up by Day as soon as he showed up. At least he distracted him so I could finish fighting Commando!

Moms tried to help. I refrained from telling her about my problems, not wanting to be seen as a "mamma's boy". However, results of blows showed up on my face and she got reports from others. Karate class came up as the answer. I was enrolled in Mr. Fierce's school, which was held in the basement of a church on the corner of Eastern Parkway and Rockaway Avenues. Karate lessons were good for me, but I quit after only a month.

I was discouraged that learning karate led to more fights. Someone spotted me going into the Church basement and saw the sign broadcasting "KARATE LESSONS" to pedestrians. Word went out and crazy Ray Ray, a nut my age who lived in the Towers, started badgering me. He kept saying, "LET'S FIGHT! LET ME SEE YOU DO KARATE." I explained karate was only for self-defense. In response, he pushed me and said, "DEFEND YOURSELF." Preprogrammed reflexes from the hours of training brought my leg up in a kick towards him. However, he caught my foot and held me in a nervous position. I grabbed onto a fence right next to us with both hands and used it to hold myself up as my other foot smashed upside his face. He let go after that and tried to rush me, only to lose. After that, I quit Karate class.

In hindsight, martial arts education was helping me. It's just that I never liked fighting. I sought to be left alone. Violence was used when trouble came my way because it seemed necessary. It was either I attacked or I'd be picked on; and being bullied was unacceptable. Since my world view was limited to the short run and karate brought more trouble my way, I dropped out.

Next moms tried to send me to school outside of Brownsville. As a freshman, she enrolled me into La Salle academy located on 2nd street and 2nd Ave, on the lower East side of Manhattan. It was an all-boys Catholic High School that had two buildings, a main and an annex, across from each other. For the first time, I was in a mostly all White student body setting. This was supposed to improve my chances of getting a better education, but things went bad.

I ended up in five fights that year at La Salle alone. One was a quick punch to the eye of some kid who pushed me from behind for GOD knows why. The other four were after school battles with a crew of Irish kids that I fought one at a time because they kept picking on me. Biology class bored me to death and I dozed off there uncontrollably every time. Meanwhile, the Irish crew made up of Rizzo, Sullivan and two others, thought it was cool to spit balls of paper at me, put signs on my back and even smack me awake. Every time I caught one of them, it was on after classes. To them it may have been practical jokes or some kind of hazing, but to me it was a series of unacceptable transgressions that needed to stop.

Despite standing up to them and winning most of the fights (3 out of 4), they didn't leave me alone until the principal got involved. Three of the rumbles were after school victories that went under the radar because no one sustained any visible damage that couldn't be wiped away. However, the last fight with Sullivan went bad for me. I ended up with a mild concussion. When moms noticed, she took me to the hospital, wrestled the truth out and raised hell at the school. From then on, I slept in biology class in peace the rest of freshman year, destined for Bishop Loughlin High School for sophomore term.

During that summer of 85, moms declared she didn't buy

teenagers' clothes and got me a job. First she took me to get working papers, then to meet Jewel, a Jerry curled southern brown skin older man with a huge 70s style moustache, who sold watermelons on busy avenues. He hired me to work for $150 a week!

The job involved real labor. We had to unload his 18 Wheeler truck full of melons at each of his several locations at the start of each day. We would form a Conga like line and toss them along to the next employee. Each one you dropped came out your pay. Then we sold the melons to whoever stopped by upon seeing our displays. At days end, we reloaded the seemingly heavier left over melons on his rig and settled up with him.

It was physically hard work and long hours in the summer heat, but I loved it for the pay. In 85, a hundred and twenty bucks a week (after deductions for watermelons that got spattered on the ground and lunch money borrowed) was huge for a 14 year old. A pair of Puma or Adidas was only $35. A pair of Calvin Klein or Lee jeans was only 20 bucks and you could see a movie for $5. That job kept me in the latest fashion.

Everything about the job was all good until a beef with some dudes from Prospect Plaza came to head. I got into an argument with some dude named Lloyd over a chick from the west building of the Towers on the phone. I had been talking to her, but he claimed to be her man and tripped on me for calling. He surprised me by coming to my apartment with his homeboy. Not expecting him, I answered the door wearing slippers and he greeted me with a punch to my mouth. I slammed the door, ran to put on my sneakers, grabbed a knife and went after him. They were still in the long hallway, but by the staircase, 30 feet away. He wouldn't come near me after I returned. They never saw the knife, but I guess they knew I must have had something to equalize the odds of 2 against 1. The standoff ended once they decided to leave, probably thinking it was better.

A few days later, I caught Lloyd by himself and stepped up to him immediately, looking to settle the score one on one, but he fessed up. He apologized claiming the girl lied on me and we shouldn't fight over her. I let it go down one punch.

Then they caught me at work on Thomas Boyland Blvd and Atlantic and tried to steal some watermelons. Traffic was moderate along the busy 6 lane Atlantic, but no pedestrians were about. Lloyd rolled up with the same homeboy from our first encounter and asked for a freebie and I said, "NO." Then they started taking them anyway. Just as I jumped up to fight them, Jewel and two of his sons pulled up in his silver Mercedes. He jumped out and threw hot coffee on Lloyd. One of Jewel's sons squared off with the other until we overwhelmed them and they ran away, but not before busting his son's nose, leaving it leaking like a water hose.

From that day on Jewel felt I was too soft to work alone. I was hurt that my courage went unrecognized. Rodney Dangerfield got more respect than me. What more could I have done than stand my ground? I finished out the summer and never returned to work for him again.

* * * * *

In the fall of 1985, I started going to Loughlin in the Clinton Hill section of Brooklyn. It was much more to my liking. The coed student body was filled with fly girls from mostly Black families and some were well off. Although there was a dress code, freedom from uniforms left room for us to dress to impress, which most of us did. Fellas rocked Clarks, Bally's or British Walkers shoes with Calvin Klein jeans and Polo or Tommy Hilfiger shirts. The chicks rocked Gucci, Liz Claiborne and Tommy too. Everybody wore fancy coats in the winter, like Jerry G goose down jackets, Sheepskins or Bubble goose leather jackets with fur around the hoods. The place was a fashion show.

There was no such thing as a boring class when compared to La Salle. Excitement could be felt just by being caught in the pull of so many attractive opposites. I hardly ever fell asleep in class again. Moreover, even when I did (Chemistry was tough on the eyes), everyone was raised smarter than to play games with a young man napping.

I started to come out of my shell there. Prior to attending Loughlin, I was pretty square. No drugs, no alcohol consumption, no girlfriends. To avoid drama, I mostly stayed inside playing video games on Atari 2600 or a Commandor 64 computer moms got us. I didn't feel accepted in my neighborhood back then and wasn't willing to follow anyone except myself. So, apart from playing baseball or riding my bike, (which someone was always trying to take), I often stayed inside. Once at Loughlin, I met people from other parts of the city and would travel as far as South Jamaica Queens to hang out. Fashion became important and I started learning what to wear, where to hang out and how to carry myself around girls.

To keep money coming in for clothes and hanging out, I got a job after school working for Spurt Messenger service in Manhattan. The messenger job paid just minimum wage and I was available only part time. At best, I brought home $70 a week.

As a side hustle, I started selling bootleg copies of video games for the Commodore 64. My boy junior worked for a company that gave him new games that I would trade with a friend at school who also had a connection. By acting as a middleman, I developed a nice collection of the hottest games, like EA sports, Dr. Jay v Larry Bird one on one basketball and others. Then I started copying them onto floppy disc for sell at $5 a pop. I didn't even think about whether it was legal or not.

Once I was swimming in the waters of cool people, dressing in Tommy this and Polo that, girls started to notice me – and so did the haters.

Seemed like everybody around the way was offering me weed all of a sudden. I refused, viewing their gestures as scams. They were always trying to pool enough money together to get high. If they got me hooked, then the next few times would be on me. After all, they hadn't been showing me any love before. Plus getting high conflicted with staying fly. I didn't make enough money to do both.

Also, somebody was always getting robbed up at Loughlin. I saw dudes headed home freezing, without coats after being jacked. A friend named Leslie, who became like a sister to me, got taken for her boyfriend's big gold rope chain. The fly freckled-faced light skin sister with a short salt-like hair dew, took it in stride, but I didn't. Not only wasn't I feeling some goons robbing her, but it was also a warning of what could happen to anybody, including me.

CHAPTER 2

In 1985, at 15 years old, I started carrying knives. There wasn't any particular event that led to that decision. When something wasn't happening to me, I either saw or heard about somebody getting victimized. Moms was robbed right in front of me at butcher knife point; Shamel got shot in his face by a .22 welding Jamaican; our apartment got burglarized 3 times; pops was murdered by a jacker and Leslie got stuckup at school. Crews, like the Deceptacons, ran the subways and street like packs of wolves hunting for prey. The volatile atmosphere led to an intense fear of getting attacked at any moment I was outside our apartment. It was that general fear of getting bum rushed and the determination not to be a helpless victim that inspired the feeling of needing to be armed when in those streets. So I started carrying kitchen steak knives wrapped in sheaths made out of paper and tape.

The first person I ever tried to kill was myself. Somehow the ghetto manipulated me into believing I was the problem. No one else was harassed as much as me. I was convinced that, as the common denominator, it was my fault people picked on me. It was my fault moms had to work all those long hours to take care of us. She always jokingly asked random strangers if they wanted to buy two kids. She said it so much that I often wondered what would happen if anybody ever replied, yes. They say there is a lot of truth in jokes. I figured my death would solve everybody's problems.

I held the knife to my wrist, ready to severe the blood vessels beneath the surface of my skin, but just couldn't do it. I couldn't cut into my own flesh. As a plan B, I took a bottle of pills from our medicine cabinet and swallowed every single one. To make sure no one found me until death did, I hid under the bed in the room Hakeem and I shared. I passed out expecting to land in the Grim Reaper's arms only to awake 16 hours later still living and feeling refreshed.

No one ever seemed to notice I had been missing, even though our small apartment only had two side by side bedrooms. My mother came home from a double shift and went right to sleep then straight back to work. Little brother was oblivious. No one ever knew I tried to kill myself and I never tried again.

Suicide was never tried again because I awoke with a realization that it wasn't my fault. Who could help being born? I never bullied anybody, so there were no karma issues. As for moms, she did what she wanted to do to get us what she wanted us to have. She strove to overcome having an alcoholic mother and divorcing our fathers. Therefore, her motivation to do so much for us was to prove something, just as much as it was out of love.

The first human being I ever stabbed was in defense of Troy Mitchell in 1985. He was an equally ghetto standard of spoiled latch key kid my age. He was a generous dude who couldn't tell anybody no and would give you the shirt off his back if you asked. Like me, he was handsome, tall and skinny with curly hair, except that his complexion is a tannish, West Indian shade. He lived on the 15th floor in my building with his aunt Bobbie who gave him $150 to go Easter Clothes shopping. I was 15 at the time, Hakeem was just turning 12 and moms gave us $150 each for Easter also.

Troy, Hakeem and I went Downtown Brooklyn to purchase outfits to wear on Easter, when we would go to the movies with a bunch of us from the Towers. Clothing and jewelry stores lined both sides of Fulton Street where crowds shopped. We went to Dr. Jays Sporting Gear store where they had team Starter jackets that were in vogue back then. Hakeem copped a white one with "SIXERS" written across the chest in blue lettering. I bought a black jacket with "CAROLINA" in burgundy colored letters. Troy got a royal blue one with "KNICKS" written on its chest in orange. We also went to another store and bought Guess jeans, which left us plenty of dough to go to the movies that Sunday.

I had some extra money from selling video games and working, so I also got a small gold rope chain. It cost $100 bucks and was the first piece of jewelry I ever owned.

After we finished shopping, Troy asked us to walk to nearby Clinton Hill to visit his folks before heading back to Brownsville. Clinton Hill was about 10 blocks through brownstone lined streets. It was a nice spring day, although chilly it was sunny and bright. We all had on bubble V goose leather coats but with only T-shirts on underneath. As we neared the apartment complex where Troy's relatives resided, a group of about 12 teenagers popped behind us. I recognized one as a guy who hung out in front of Loughlin. He stood out to me because his face was brunt and he usually had on a Gilligan's type hat. He always looked like he was up to no good.

At first the crew's intentions weren't clear. They surrounded and separated us while making bogus trade offers. A dark skin guy about my size and age, wearing a leather jacket offered to trade a fur hat he was wearing for my thin, but solid 14 karat gold rope chain. Of course I refused to swap the $100 rope for a beat up $20 used "fur" hat, but he kept on trying to convince me it was a great deal. Next thing I knew, Troy was tug-a-warring over his Dr. Jay shopping bag containing his newly purchased Starter jacket. The 5 or 6 teenagers who were trying to intimidate Hakeem and I, abandoned us and bum-rushed Troy. They had him on the ground, kicking and stomping my friend right in front of me while he continued to hold on to his bags. I froze up in fear and shock as Troy was being pummeled and robbed.

As I stood there forgotten, seeing Troy kicked by someone's Timberland boot snapped me out of the stupor. I was able to draw my knife and run up behind the pack of wolves preying on my boy. As hard as I could, I stabbed the closest one to me in the back of his head. He just happened to be the smallest of them, at about 5 feet 5 inches! The blade didn't penetrate his skull, instead it slid down the back of his head, deeply ripping flesh in its way from crown to an inch above the nape of his neck. When he screamed in pain his whole crew stopped smashing on Troy and looked towards me with murderous intent.

There was no doubt in my mind that the knife was not going to stop all of them from rushing me and taking it. Thinking fast, I instantly slammed my weapon to the pavement and started zipping down my jacket with my left, while reaching inside with my right. Acting as if there was a gun concealed, I yelled, "YALL WANT TO PLAY, LET"S PLAY!" Having every reason to believe my bluff, their crew scattered in all directions. Unfortunately, the Dr. Jay's bag broke leaving Troy with the plastic handle part and one of the fleeing assailants with the brand new Knicks Starter.

Troy was grateful not to have received any more kicks and for not losing his Guess jeans or remaining money. Neither he nor Hakeem noticed I had frozen up like a statue for a few precious seconds, allowing the attack to go further than it had to.

That experience cemented justification for carrying a knife to me. If I didn't have it, we would have all been robbed or worse. Moreover, I learned the need to react without hesitation. Hesitation gave them a chance to get Troy's jacket and a few more kicks in. Had the wolf pack been more organized, they could have gotten Hakeem and I as well. Had they been more vicious, Troy could have been getting stabbed, instead of just beat.

* * * * *

While growing up, our uncle Boo Boo was our male role model. He always looked out for his older sisters and us. He would come around and give both single mother siblings money as well as us. He usually had a good job and was friends with the singer Steve, who sung "Set it off." Boo Boo, born Zach Thomas, would sleep over on the weekends from time to time and taught us valuable lessons.

A major thing I learned from him that became imbedded in my personality was knowing the difference between playtime and serious moments. The 5'11 medium built twenty something year old would take on all of us playing fighting. DeAngelo, Hakeem and myself would have a ball jumping Uncle Boo Boo and often didn't want to quit. He would warn us that once he was tired and said that's it, playtime was over. Anybody who kept on after his announcement got punched in the arm for real. Caught up in the rapture of fun time, it was hard to stop playing so suddenly. After a couple of those grown man hits, I learned to abruptly stop when playtime was instantly over. To this day, I can switch from happy go lucky mode to dead serious as instantly as circumstances require.

One day Boo Boo stopped coming around. Moms cursed him out for smoking weed in the house while we were there. I never saw it. She caught him and pitched a fit. That slowed down his visits. However losing his job at the telephone company and becoming a drug addict completed the vanishing act. By 1985, when the streets started getting their craziest, nobody was there to guide me on how to cope.

In the absence of an actual male role model, Dr. Spock filled the void. Instead of drowning in emotional turmoil from stabbing that teenager, I sought out logic. I developed a rationalization that cutting that jacker was something needed to be done once playtime was over.

Calling the police seemed "illogical" because you could only get their help after it was too late, if at all. The police couldn't make your injuries go away, bring back anyone to life and likely wouldn't get your property back once taken. In fact, the system would put you through more stresses by having you go through books of mug shots, victim services, several interviews, a line-up and many court dates. All that just to see your attacker either beat the case, get a light sentence or get a harshly long one at tax payers' expense. Plus, ain't no witness protection program for a state case; but a weapon could be there in the heat of the moment. It could nip problems in the bud on the spot by reversing the role of victim into victor.

Fighting with my hands seemed like it wasn't enough to reach the desired goal of being left alone. Despite standing my ground against all comers, I had to fight the same people over and over again. Commando and I had 4 bouts, 3 of which I won. I fought Hassan 7 times until I finally beat him. I fought our worst hood bully, Omar (14 Mike Tyson shaped loon) twice going 1 and 1. Somebody was always trying to take something from me, if not my bike than my sense of self-worth and they didn't mind losing another fight to try again. However, they left alone anyone they thought was crazy enough to kill them.

Psychologically, I needed weapons the way Lunis from the Peanuts cartoon needed his blue security blanket. Armed with a sharp instrument, I felt secure and confident that bullies older than me; and always being outnumbered could be dealt with. Without a weapon, I felt like a helpless deer hoping no tigers rolled up when that's inevitable since we all resided in the same jungle. In them streets, a weapon was the only thing I had to rely on.

I was alone against the world. My childhood buddies, another Troy (Taylor) moved when we were 9 and Mutar, when we were 15. I had no crew and no help against the outside world. The police policy was to let them kill each other. They were never around when you needed them and didn't put much enthusiasm into solving Black on Black crimes, calling them "NHI" for "No Humans Involved."

I didn't have any faith in GOD. Although I learned all about the Almighty and Jesus from the Catholic Schools attended, I saw no signs of GOD in Brownsville. The existence of a Brownsville alone proved to me that any GOD that existed cared as little about me as some say the second president Bush cared about the victims of Hurricane Katrina.

My mother still sent us to church on Sundays, even though she was too tired to go herself. I went there and fell asleep during the one hour service, thankful they were over fast. GOD to me was an imaginary friend who I talked to in times of need, but who never appeared to answer back.

Once sharp objects became my protector, I stopped using kitchen utensils and got a butterfly knife. It was silver, with a line of factory made holes on both sides of the handles. When manipulated correctly, it unleashes a 5 inch dagger like blade. I practiced until it could be drawn, extending its sharp edge, at Billy the Kid speeds. Whenever I left the comfort of my living room, my right hand was in my right front pocket, clutching the knife, as if it doubled as a lucky charm.

Stabbing foes became a regular occurrence. Next, that very summer of 85, I stabbed Daddy O. He was about 3 years older than me and was still in high school while I was getting ready to start my junior year. All the youngsters around the way looked up to him and followed his lead. The 6-3 inch tall, slim, cinnamon brown skin young man kept instigating against me. He still loved calling me "Whiteboy" in that hateful tone of voice, encouraging others to do the same.

On the night in question, we were working at our summer job in Brooklyn's Coney Island at the ring toss booth. It was across from the Himalaya ride and down the block from Nathan's Famous Franks. Our job was to sell 5 chances to win a huge stuffed animal for $1 by throwing a plastic ring and hoping it lands on top of a bottle. "Daddy O" had owed me $5 dollars for a few weeks and after we got paid, I asked for it. His response was crazy. He said he wasn't going to give me anything unless I fought for it. Assuming I wanted to fight, he took off his shirt and then started talking trash on the way to the train station. It was past 11:00 pm when we reached the deserted Stillman Avenue subway stop, where we often went to avoid paying the fare to ride the F train to the A train home. About five other youths from the Towers who worked with us were there too, but no one tried to stop him.

When we got to the empty parking lot in front of the long stairway to the elevated train platform, Daddy O got into a boxer's stance. Meanwhile, my butterfly knife was already extended and hidden behind my waist. There was no way I was going to fight fair against someone 50lb heavier and 3 years older over $5 measly bucks I was nice enough to lend him. Especially since he earned the ability to repay with the job I got him. I was scared and hated him for all the times he called me "Whiteboy" and provoked others to fight me. I felt angry that my reward for looking out for him was supposed to be getting beat up. As fear turned to anger, hatred turned to rage, I lunged at him as soon as he tried to swing at me. He saw the metal dagger coming and deflected it in a nick of time to keep it from going deep enough to cause a critical injury, but his wrist paid the price. It was sliced open to the white meat, absorbing most of the blunt force of my blow. However, the tip of the blade barely poked into his abdomen, leaving a shallow hole. Surprised, he backed off quickly, yelling, "HE STABBED ME, THAT MOTHER[S]UCKER STABBED ME!" I didn't push the issue once he got the point.

While others helped Daddy O, I headed up the long staircase to the El train platform. The train didn't come fast enough, as it ran slow during off peak hours. Daddy O came up on the platform with the others right as the locomotive pulled into the station. From a half of platform distance, he stared at me with malice in his eyes as we boarded different cars of the same train. It was about a 45 minutes ride to Jay St., where we would transfer to the A train for the 30 minute ride to Rockaway Ave. That's a long time to dodge someone.

Daddy O came after me. He ran from one car to the next in-between stops because the doors connecting the cars were all locked. I saw him coming with a broken bottle in the shape of a make-shift knife in hand. Therefore, I advanced from car to car in an effort to avoid him. I found a cop on the train and sat near him. Daddy O saw the cop near me and left the issue alone for the moment. He didn't even try to press charges or tell the police, and neither did I. What happened was between us.

Before ever reading Sun Tz, I understood the principle that you never give an enemy a 50/50 chance with your life. You pick the terms of battle. In this case, I didn't think a fight where we were both armed was fair since he was taller and stronger. Therefore, there was no way I was going to engage in a fight where the chances were in his favor, unless my back was up against a wall. Yeah, I was scared of him and of the fact that I escalated the beef to the use of life threatening weapons.

I lost Daddy O switching to the A train and made it home safe. I didn't have to work in Coney Island until the next weekend, so I sought to avoid Daddy O, at least till then. Even though we lived in the same building, it was easy because I didn't go outside much. Meanwhile, Hakeem did.

One day during that week, he was outdoors in front of our building when 3 older guys started horse playing with him. One of them was the notorious "Purple', who liked men and had just came home from prison. He was so dark he looked purple and at 25 years old, had no business playing with my 12 year old brother. Moreover, Commando was also involved. Then there was Bee Mack, a short and dark-skinned 18- year-old cat, with curly hair and a gold tooth, who was known for being fast with his hands and fighting dirty. They caught little bro out there alone.

I supposed they were just clowning around with Hakeem until $75 dollars left over from clothes shopping fell out of his pocket. Bee Mack grabbed the money and all three of them ran down the brownstone lined Pacific street in broad daylight with Hakeem's cash. Since Hakeem knew those guys and thought they were kidding, he awaited their return. He stood there for hours before realizing they weren't corning back with his money.

I loved my little brother and there was no way I would let them get away with the robbery. More important to me was protecting him from going through what I did. I had well over 100 fights and had been jumped 3 or 4 times. Hakeem was not going to suffer the same trials, if I could help it. I was out to set the example that everybody better leave my little brother alone or else.

I grabbed another knife from among the utensils lined up in their plastic holding tray slots within a kitchen drawer. Then I went looking for the opportunist, despite Daddy O's looking for me. I circled the block for a while, but they were long gone. Too angry to add up the odds of three against one, or the Daddy O factor, I hunted them, as if determination and rage could conquer all when accompanied by steel. Round and round the area I paced until it became obvious they weren't to be found that evening.

Meanwhile Hakeem told our mother what happened to the shopping money she had given him. Since she didn't have more to replace it, along with paying our private schools' tuitions, rent and all, moms called Hakeem's father Willie. She hoped he would give his son, who I don't remember him ever coming to see, some dough to make up for what was taken. Willie had different ideas.

He showed up to our apartment looking like a Vietnam vet in army fatigues and with a heavy set beastly friend. Willie was like a brown skin version of my pops, with the same big curly afro and glasses. This was the first and only time I ever remember seeing Hakeem's dad. After Hakeem told him what happened, instead of reimbursement he went after Purple.

Purple lived on the 9th floor with a 50 something year old gay man, while his mother, sister and three brothers lived on the 22nd. Willie and his buddy used their correctional officers' badges to bluff Purple into believing he was being arrested by two detectives. They went into Purple's love next and took him out in handcuffs. Once they got him into an awaiting van, they drove him somewhere and beat his butt until he promised to repay the money and never bother Hakeem again. Then they dropped him back at the Towers. Purple never did harass us again.

That left Bee Mack and Commando up to me. A few days later, I saw Bee Mack out in front of the Towers from my terrace just as it was getting dark. Immediately, I grabbed an aluminum bat, hid it in my pants and under my T-shirt and went out to see him with the not-so-concealed weapon. While clutching the Louisville Slugger, I ran up on Bee Mack, ready to pull it out, but as I approached, he indicated that he just wanted to talk. I held off attacking to listen.

Bee Mack apologized for his part and gave me back $50 of what they took. He told me they were just joking, but once they got away with the money they decided to get some weed and go the deuce (pre Gulilani 42nd St) to see some Kung Fu flicks. He admitted he was wrong in a sincere tone and said it was up to the others to pay back the rest. I believe he had just scored big that day because he was wearing two gold rings on every finger and had a pocketful full of money all of a sudden. Anyway, all was forgiven and forgotten with Bee Mack.

Commando was another story. He made a whole bunch of excuses as to why he wasn't going to give us back anything. However, he worked in Coney Island with me during weekends so I decided to wait till he got paid to take Hakeem's loot back. To poor people, recovery is more important than revenge.

On that Saturday, after we got paid, Commando walked around the amusement park spending my brother's money on video games, cotton candy, hot dogs and pizza. As we only made about $35 bucks a day, I feared it would be all eaten up before I could retrieve it. With crowds of unsuspecting people everywhere, I had to wait until the routine route home through the quiet Stillman Avenue train station to make a move.

Daddy O didn't show up to work that day, so he was one less thing to worry about. Still, that situation was far from over.

When night fell and we headed towards Stillman, Commando was clueless that something was amiss. I thought that maybe I gave off a harmless aura because guys who should know better hardly ever took me seriously. It was as if he thought robbing Hakeem was no big deal.

As soon as we got to the secluded area under the EL, I attacked. I socked him with a right, landing a flush punch upside his temple and reached into his pocket for Hakeem's dough. He was my age and I had beaten him in several fair fights in the past, so there was no plan to use my ever hardy butterfly knife. Plans changed once I got into trouble.

I had gotten close to Commando and the battle became a wrestling match. With him being 20 pounds heavier, plus stronger, I ended up in a headlock. Instinctively striving for survival, I resorted to slipping the knife from my pocket and stabbing him in his rear-end to make him release me from his air choking grip. He screamed in pain and as he went to run, I ripped Hakeem's money from his pocket. All he had left was $18 bucks.

The next day, while I was working in Coney Island, both Commando and Daddy O showed up and neither of them came to work. They were both armed with 007 blades which was the biggest "pocket" knife sold. It was like carrying a foldable butcher's knife.

They messed up trying to get me at our job site. They should have waited until I got back to Brownsville. While Coney Island seemed like just a fun amusement park to the unaware, it is located near a few housing projects. Gangs like the 40 thieves use to run the boardwalk at night and robbery was common. My cousin DeAngelo was the one who started going out there first. His twin friends, Tony and Eric, put him on at their sister Susan's ring toss booth which their family had owned out there for years. I brought everyone from the Towers out. None of them had the juice DeAngelo, Tony and Eric had in that part of Brooklyn.

As I spent the day staying in crowded areas and watching my back, word went out that Daddy O and Commando were after me and why. Just when they had me alone by the boardwalk under a dust sky, about 12 Coney Island natives came to my rescue. As Daddy O and Commando were following me, CI's underworld was watching them. With the situation flipped, I could have had them smashed, but I knew we had to live in Brownsville together and all I wanted was to squash the beefs. Under duress, they agreed to leave me alone.

I didn't believe Daddy O was sincere about squashing the beef until the following weekend. He had gotten jumped by a bunch of weight lifting Italians while Commando was nowhere to be seen from what I heard. Gremlin, from our building, was the one who stayed and fought on his side. When the police came, they arrested Daddy O instead of the Italians, even though his face was swollen, proving he was attacked. Meanwhile, the Italians waited outside the precinct for Daddy O, as if they had diplomatic immunity.

When Gremlin came and got me, I put aside the prior beef and went to check on him. After all, being Black came before anything else and the incident had racial overtones.

The Italians were about 5 deep. They all looked like Lou Ferrigno type dudes, with spiky flat tops and Mullet hair-dos. They were grown men in their early twenties. They seemed angry, as if Daddy O beat them up, and acted ready to tear him apart when he reemerged. The police going in and out the station house ignored us.

Gremlin, only 13, short and skinny as hell, armed himself with a brick to make up the difference. He had it barely hidden behind his right leg as we awaited Daddy O on the opposite side of the precinct's front steps from the Italians. Gremlin was known as such because he got into trouble running the streets all hours of the night after his mom got strung out on crack and his pops left. He was always down for whatever.

I don't know if the Italians got tired of waiting or were worried about us. Although we were only skinny teenagers, clearly out matched physically, we weren't scared of them. We stood there staring, as if our looks could kill them. They may have thought we had a gun or were too young to fight because all they did was curse us out and leave. They even ignored Gremlin challengingly throwing his brick at them. When Daddy O was released a few minutes after, I think he appreciated us being there for him. Over the years, he had many chances to get me back but has never even tried.

Commando was a totally different story. The thug, who robbed my brother and tried to kill me, actually pressed charges! About a week or two after he was stabbed, the police from the Coney Island precinct came and arrested me for assault with a deadly weapon and armed robbery. I made no statements and mentally prepared for the trip to the notorious Riker's Island with indifference. Luckily, before the booking process could be completed, I was released from their filthy holding cell. Commando dropped the charges when he found out, if he didn't, he would be on the Island along with me for jacking Hakeem

.

* * * * *

As I became more outgoing, clubbing became my thing. Our spot was Union Square, where body builder security guards didn't seem to notice most of us weren't 18. Hip Hop music blasted from their speakers and there was always a dance floor packed with teenage girls and danger.

Every week we would save our money to go. Lane, (a buddy from Coney Island who could dance his tail off), DeAngelo, Hakeem (who at 12 looked older than me at the time), and I would go together. We practiced dances, like the "Pee Wee Herman", "Running Man" and "Bizmark", so no female would out-do us. Rakim, Ultra Magnetic MCs, Audio Two, Mc Lyte, Biz Markie, LL Cool J, Run Dee MC, and other Hip Hop legends kept the party rocking. We just couldn't get enough.

There was drama at the club every time we went. I would sneak razor blades inside for protecting us, but it never came to that. It was always someone else who was beat-up when security cut the lights on and stopped the music. The trouble makers would get thrown out, messed quickly cleaned up, then the music would restart and we'd resume partying as if nobody just got bum-rushed, robbed and cut.

Moms always said, if you need a weapon to go there, then you don't need to go. But we were too addicted to that music and chasing girls to stay away. Besides, I didn't think anywhere was safe without a weapon on me. Violence was part of the only life I knew.

CHAPTER 4

"HE THOUGHT HE HAD A SMOOTH BROTHER GOT, BUT THE SMOOTH BROTHER GOT HIM" –NAS

The next drama that unfolded caused a breakdown between moms and me. One night she sent me to Consumers for bleach. She needed it to wash her white shirts for work, as she was a captain by then. She insisted I go to Consumers because it was cheaper than the Bodega across the street.

I didn't want to go to Consumers because it was a longer walk. Plus it was in a dimly lit area within Atlantic Towers' grounds, halfway between the East and West buildings. Meanwhile, the Bodega was directly across the street on the well-lit Rockaway Avenue with traffic going back and forth. However, I went to Consumers as ordered.

I put on my leather ¾ length coat with the fur around the hood. Although my mother bought it for me the year before, it still looked new. There was a rug cutter in the right hand pocket for my protection. I had thrown the butterfly blade away after the Commando incident, knowing better than to keep a used weapon.

It was a cold and deserted night. It had to be before 7:30pm because that's when Consumers closed, yet it was already pitch black outside. The cloudy winter sky blocked out moonlight, creating an even more shadow embracing darkness. I passed no one in my hurried pace on the sidewalk pathway behind and on the side of the Towers to the grocery store. A leeriness had me clutching the heavy metal carpet cutter.

It was quick and easy to buy the bleach and leave. There were only a few shoppers inside the brightly lit store that shined like a light house through the inky night. Making it home with that bleach was another story.

Just as I passed the well-lit area within range of the lighted store into the shadows along its side, a teenager, with a nasty limp approached me. He menacingly ordered, "RUN YOUR COAT." The dark skin jacker was half crippled and skeletal skinny. There was a stocky guy wearing a sheepskin coat that appeared to be with him, but he stood about 20 feet away with his back against the shaded side of Consumers, as if hiding. The one who came up on me was Grasshopper from Prospect Plaza, the notorious projects on nearby Saratoga Avenue whose residents I kept getting into it with.

I viewed the seemingly handicapped would-be jacker with a body like Paris Hilton as no threat and smirked while continuing to walk away. Pissed off at being ignored, he hopped to catch up and showed a Gem Star single edge razor blade. Then he told me, "I'M SERIOUS, RUN YOUR COAT."

Thinking fast, I replied, "ALRIGHT, ALRIGHT, YOU GOT IT," in a fearful tone.

I stooped over to my left to put the bag of bleach on the ground and slipped the rug cutter out with my right hand. While he was distracted watching the harmless bag, I sliced his neck open. Not knowing what the other guy would do, I backed up 30 feet into the lighted view of Consumers' employees and few remaining customers. That way they could see me through the huge front windows and provide, or at least call, help if things got uglier than I could handle.

I challenged them, yelling, "COME ON, COME GET IT!" Instead, Grasshopper grabbed his neck with one hand, my bag in his other and ran in the opposite direction. The mysterious guy in the sheepskin followed behind him.

Upon coming home empty handed, my mother insisted on me hurrying straight back to Consumers before it closed. For the first time in years I broke the anti-momma's boy and opened up willingly about what had just happened. I clearly explained that there was danger they would return. I pleaded that if she needed to send me back out, at least let me go to the Bodega across the street. She didn't take the incident serious and I was sent straight back into the dangerous night.

I hoped Grasshopper was too injured to return, at least that night. Still he could send others from Prospect Plaza to kill me on his behalf. Therefore I dreaded the nervous walk around the building, back into the shadows to reach Consumers.

On the way I found Billy, a 12 year old kid, walking his dog. He was enlisted on my mission. His dog was only a cute little Benji looking mutt, but both of them and the rug cutter were all I had. As we neared the store's east gate, I could see five males approaching from the west.

From Guns to God

One of them was walking with a hop and that was all I needed to see. Billy and I did a u-turn and ran for the safety of our building and its front security locking doors. We had a huge lead which made the chase no contest.

When I went upstairs empty handed again, my mother gave me an earful. However, I refused to go back outside and she just had to make do.

The following day, a correctional officer who lived in the Towers saved my life. I was laughing and joking with Toofy, a sports fanatic who also both lived in the building and went to Loughlin one grade ahead of me. We were coming down the ½ block long pathway to our complex and made it without any event. When I arrived upstairs, my mother was home with a big muscular man and who told me how close I came to death.

The correction officer saw Grasshopper suspiciously hiding in the bushes near the entrance to the Towers. He said Grasshopper was too focused on me as I headed obliviously towards danger. Feeling something was going on, he snuck up on Grasshopper, grabbed him from behind and took a loaded gun from his person. Grasshopper broke free and ran off without his gun. The correction officer warned me to be careful.

Now moms started to take my fears of the streets seriously. However, she was confused as to what the issues really were. She assumed I must be selling drugs in order to have that murder 1 level type of beef. In her day, you didn't have to worry about getting shot unless you were out there living like that. So she had some guy give Hakeem and I an hour long lecture on not selling drugs and staying out of trouble. I couldn't relate to none of his jibber jabber because I sold copied video games, not drugs. I had three leather coats and two suede fronts, but my mother purchased them all for me. There was no unexplained surplus of cash. My so called "criminal acts," were acts of survival. I only carried weapons because of a refusal to allow the concrete jungle to prey on me. He didn't give us any advice on how to be left alone. The only thing he did was insult us with false implications of being drug dealers.

That same night my mother sent me to me store for bleach again! This time I was going to Bodega, even though that meant paying the difference in price from Consumers. I took an utility knife with me, which was an orange-colored plastic case containing a long razor blade that came up with a slide of my thumb. It made a click, click sound as its blade extended and became the popular weapon of choice for adolescent wars in New York City. Even though I hoped for the best, I was prepared for the worst.

Inside the small Bodega, many products competed, jammed together, for shelf space, however the Clorox bleach was easy to find. It did have a layer of dust on the bottle, as if no one had purchased bleach from there in years. But it was the same bleach, just 30 cents more.

When I exited the store, Grasshopper was waiting for me. I thought he had another gun and came to shoot me, so I ran to the nearest parked car. Then I circled a white Toyota to keep it as shelter between us. I hoped the cover would protect me as Grasshopper took what felt like forever to pull something long out of his cheap blue cotton coat. I feared it must be a long barreled .357, by how high he raised his hand above his waist line as he pulled it out. What materialized was a very long butcher knife. When I saw that was it, I drew my razor and extended the sharp edge, prepared to stand and fight. Then I thought, why should I? Here was this dirty looking bum with a bigger knife than I had. Meanwhile I had too much to lose and a huge disadvantage, so I jetted to the building as he hopelessly hopped after me.

As soon as I got home, I called DeAngelo for help. He wasn't a thug or goon but he looked the part. His answer to Brownsville bullies was to lift weights. Doing so made him look big, muscular and, with his hair in cornrow braids and a BVD thin nylon t-shirt showing off results, he had an intimidating presence. Although a gentle giant, he would ride for his family. As he only lived 10 blocks away, he walked over to spend the night and escort me to school the next day.

When morning came, we headed down Rockaway Avenue to Fulton, hoping to avoid trouble, but ready for the worst. On the way to the A train station, we ran into Wise, my cousin, Angel's ex-boyfriend. He had just come home from prison and was trying to do the right thing with his life. The brown skin pretty boy had wavy hair, a prison physique and the devil's smile. He had to take the train to work, so we recruited him to roll with us.

Also along were Toofy and Trey from the Towers who went to

Loughlin as well. Both were known for defying physics when it came to drama. They occupied space but didn't matter because neither would do anything. Still, it looked good to the unaware to appear five deep.

Seeing Grasshopper again was inevitable with our buildings three blocks apart, but I thought it would be in the evening, like all the other times. The extra people that morning were a precaution, a precaution I'm glad we took. As soon as I got to the bottom of the stairs into the subway station, Grasshopper was standing beside the token booth, waiting.

By his sides were two big menace-looking grown men with sheepskin coats on. Both looked like they had done hard time. Luckily, Wise knew one of the goons from inside. On my behalf, he negotiated a one on one fight to settle the issues between us once and for all. I was blessed to have DeAngelo and Wise with me that day --- otherwise, things might have gone differently.

I agreed to shoot the fair one, took off my leather coat and handed it to DeAngelo. Grasshopper and I squared off in front of the token booth and turnstiles with about 40 people pressed up against them to watch the street match.

My style of fighting was no nonsense. I kept my guards up, chin down and feet moving. Grasshopper fought like a lot of Brownsville fighters, with a focus on style instead of results. He got off first, with a punch that glued the braces on my teeth into my lips, ripping flesh halfway through. I could feel shredded pieces flopping around inside my mouth. I responded mixing karate blocks in with combinations that left his eye and nose bloody. Only minutes later, we were both tired, dropping blood and had had enough. The fight ended with handshakes and that was that.

I still went to school. Stephanie helped clean my mouth up on the train ride to Lafayette Avenue station. Stephanie, a pretty yellow sister, who had extremely huge breast for a 16 year old female so slim, went to Loughlin also. We met up on the subway platform and rode to school together most mornings. After school, we hung out at each other's houses a lot. I started off wanting to date her but somehow we ended up only being friends. We claimed to be siblings to explain to people we did dated why we spent so much time together.

Just a few weeks later, I got into drama walking to the Lafayette from Loughlin with Steph. She had two friends with her, Maysoon and

Sally. Maysoon is an orangey complexioned sister who had cheek length hair, bubble-shaped eyes and a beautiful smile on a thick, nicely built frame. Sally had my vote for prettiest chick in our whole school. She resembled a shorter, thicker, younger version of the actress Sally Richardson. As I gladly escorted the hot young ladies to the subway, trouble rolled up.

A guy named Cat came up from behind with five other guys and started strolling along with us. He started flirting with Maysoon and squeezed her booty. At first I was ready to speak up on her behalf and check sun about his disrespectful act. However, when all Maysoon did was smile, giggle and say "stoooopppppp!" in a half-hearted way, I hoped they were cool like that. Truth is, we were all leery of Cat.

Cat lived in Clinton Hill near Loughlin and used to go there too. He was thrown out by Mr. Dorney, an ex-deductive turned principle. Cat was tall and thin, with a complexion like Maysoon, but freckled and he wore a low haircut. When school let out, he would often be in front at the same time with a bunch of strange dudes, who no one knew. He would mingle with whoever had something he felt worth taking. Then whoever he chatted with got robbed by the strangers, right after Cat's timely walk off.

That day he was with some dangerous looking dudes. One guy had a Flattop and a long keloid scar on the side of his face. It went from his temple to his chin. I had seen the scar-faced teen with another whose facial area was two-toned and wrinkly, probably from being brunt. He was involved in that incident where I sliced someone to save Troy. Maybe that was why they tried what they tried next, however, no one ever explained their reasoning.

One minute Cat was kicking his game, the next he was telling the young ladies to, "GO ON AHEAD CAUSE THIS MUST BE DONE." I didn't understand what the hell he meant, but it didn't sound good, so I clutched the utility knife hidden in my right pocket, ready to cut on the side of caution. The girls didn't ask any clarifying questions, they just hurried ahead and left me to fend for myself, six to one.

That didn't seem fair. Whatever happened to women's lib? I would have helped if six chicks came to jump them. Yet they practically ran off.

Suddenly Cat swung at me. Already prepared, his punch was easily side stepped. I drew my razor in response and ripped through the air at his chest. He backed up, then his crew started to converge. I kept swinging the deadly blade to keep them at bay. It only slowed them down. They would back up a step then keep coming after avoiding my weapon's reach. I kept swinging and backing up with each of their advances, all the way down the block, down the subway steps and all the way to the token booth. A transit officer was down there and his presence inspired them to abandon the attempted attack.

The following day, I brought a butcher knife to school in another made up sheath. A razor wasn't good enough against multiple attackers because its effect wasn't always immediately felt in the heat of combat. However, a well-placed knife stab would sit an attacker down. Really, I hoped to avoid further drama all together, but that wasn't up to me.

That very morning, Cat was crossing the street headed directly towards me from the front of Loughlin. He was all by himself. I intended to just walk on by, but he was staring at me with malice in his eyes. I felt equal hatred towards him and stared right back as we were going by each other. Just as he was almost completely passed, he said, "WHAT!"

"WHAT!" I responded. His reply to that was pulling out a utility knife, exactly like the one I had the day before. This time, I drew a butcher knife from my waist band and we squared off blade against blade.

For some reason, people always misjudged me. My awkward appearance and clumsiness gave many the wrong impression. They thought I was soft. Though being underestimated, I often overachieved. People who took the perception for the reality learned their error the hard way.

Like the others, Cat foolishly gave me an opening that I took with no hesitation. He paused in the middle of our knife dance, dropped his guard and asininely asked, "WHAT ARE YOU GOING TO DO WITH THAT?" I guess he believed I wouldn't use it.

His answer was a lunge, plunging the mini sword into his chest/shoulder area. Abruptly, Mr. Dorney came out of the school right as I was withdrawing the knife from Cat's slender body. Somehow, he was still on his feet, dripping blood, as we both hid our weapons. When I headed for the school entrance, Cat didn't follow. Mr. Dorney didn't seem to notice what had gone down under his nose.

Once inside the building, I passed the knife off to Toofy and made my way to class like nothing happened. Violence became as commonplace as in a Loony Tunes Cartoon where I come from.

Mr. Dorney looked like a detective and still had those skills. He wore his hair in a DA haircut, with a big brushy mustache on an otherwise clean face. His young looks didn't match the color of his sandy gray and white hair. He wore a gray suit, like a detective and was rumored to carry a .38 caliber revolver.

By the end of the day, he had called me to his office. When I got there, it wasn't hard to tell what for. He had my knife sitting on his desk. Along with it were four students, including Toofy, Shelton, Trevor, and two active detectives to boot, in his office. Every student there had passed the blade along throughout that day. My heart raced as the dooming scene filled my head with reasons to fear.

Mr. Dorney wasn't out to get me though. He never asked any incriminating questions and made it clear he knew what happened already. He wanted Cat, not me. It was rumored that friends of Cat's jumped Mr. Dorney before and took his gun for throwing him out of Loughlin.

Mr. Dorney was still upset because I couldn't give him anything to build a case against Cat with. He never actually hit me on either occasion yet I stabbed him with a butcher knife. Plus there was no proof he was behind all the robberies.

Meanwhile, I had a big problem to overcome if I hoped to make it home safely. I was trapped inside the school because Cat had over 50 hostile teenagers awaiting outside. I didn't have the juice Cat had to summon an army--I was on my own.

While refusing to give me a ride home, one detective joked they should let me go out there, that way they could arrest Cat while he participated in my killing. I didn't think they were so funny.

My fellow Loughlinites were allowed to leave, as I remained behind for a couple of hours, trying to out-wait the crowd. Classes let out at 2:00 pm, yet it was around 4 pm before most of the mob broke camp. Determined and unmoving, Burnt face, Scar face and Cat remained 15 feet from the door where I had to exit from.

In addition to Cat and his band of hold outs, Paco, Sally's older brother was out there too. He often went crazy in her defense. He is Trinidadian, with straight black hair and a medium built. He had quit school to sell drugs and from what I heard, he was known as a gun-blazing mad man when provoked. From Dorney's office window, I saw him sitting on the hood of his white Cadillac wearing a tricolor Polo jacket. It was as though he was waiting for me too. Remembering that Sally was at the first incident, I figured Paco wasn't with Cat.

I took the chance of coming out and asking Paco for a ride home. He agreed, as if that was why he was waiting there in the first place. Neither Cat nor any of his remaining people tried anything as I got into the back of Paco's Caddy. Some other guy was already sitting in the front passenger's seat.

On the drive home, I begin to fear a setup, as he took me on a hood tour of Bedford Stuyvesant. He stopped and visited some guy named Nut, who had a flattop haircut, big dookey gold rope chain and solid, heavy looking nugget gold bracelets on. Then we stopped here and there while he jumped out and left me in the car with his homeboy, a stranger who at no time said a word to me.

I thought Paco was going to deliver me into the hands of my enemies. After all, Paco and I weren't that close. My association with him was mostly through Toofy, Sally and Shelton who also went to Loughlin and lived in the Towers. Thinking back, he probably wanted to impress and recruit me, after hearing what I did.

Going back to Loughlin was a dead issue. Mr. Dorney gave me a "safely transfer," sparring my scholastic record the details of a stabbing. So I was out of school for a few weeks. Junior year would be continued at August Martin High School in Queens.

Excerpt from Jeffrey Little's soon-to-be-released book "Redemption for the Wicked: Part 1"

CHAPTER 1

It was almost the middle of July and it was turning out to be one of the hottest and most miserable months the small city of La Mesa, California had seen in a long time. Barely ten in the morning and the temperature remained at a steady blaze of 102 degrees.

Summer had arrived and it showed no sign of relenting or going away. The skies continued to be a soft, baby blue, without clouds. Wishing for rain was about as futile as wishing for the California budget crisis to suddenly disappear, along with the corrupt politicians who ran the state.

Bordering the outskirts of San Diego, La Mesa was a small suburb that was growing and with the expansion came the unwanted. Thieves, murderers and rapists made living in the city sort of hazardous.

Inside of the seedy, four storied Easy 8 motel room, lay a wanted man, who fit the profile of being a killer. He lay semiconscious under a strong force of refrigerated air, tossing and turning in his sleep. The cooling unit fought valiantly against the overpowering heat that loomed just outside the door, keeping the occupants of the room, cool and comfortable.

Still, a light film of perspiration covered the man's body as he battled a murky demon in his sleep. His eyes fluttered, but consciousness evaded his tormented mind. He began to moan as though he was in pain. In his world, it was very dark and the evil from his past deeds seemed to sift through his body like ash through a grill.

He was about to give in to the encompassing gloom of the dead, and then he saw her. A girl about 6 or 7, with light skin, long ringlets of dark hair and an unsettling set of Jade green eyes that gave the child a look of maturity way beyond her tender age.

Her laughter filled his ears as she gazed upon him. He smiled in return and for a brief moment of time, he was happy. Then he opened his mouth to ask the girl her name. Suddenly, the disease of the wicked entered his mouth, filling his body and chocking him with the most abhorrent taste he'd ever been forced to endure.

At the same time, a strange white hand emerged from the darkness and grasped the girl around her ankle. With fear embedded in her eyes, she screamed, "Dadddyyy! Save me! Please don't let 'em take me away!"

With fear also in the man's eyes, he reached down through the surrounding evil, straining, trying to seize the girl's hand. His fingers skimmed over the outstretched digits and instantly, the beautiful little girl disappeared from sight so fast, it was as if she'd never been there. She was gone. However, the last words she screamed, haunted the man. Her begging to be saved, played over and over in his unconscious mind.

The man's lips moved in his sleep as he tried to call out to the child. Yet, in his nightmare, he could no longer breathe. His hands jerked up towards his neck, clutching at his throat, while the little girl's pleas echoed in his ears.

Eddie Strange was suddenly awake. He immediately began to panic believing he was still in his dream-state and that wasn't a good sign for him. He took a deep breath and began to calm down, the cool air washing over his body, drying his sweat while lowering his temperature.

Eddie was a heroin user. Because of his constant abuse of the strong narcotic, a veil of mucus had formed over his eyes and dried. It made it extremely hard for him to open his eyes. He was in the process of rubbing the crust from them, when a remnant of his horrible dream re-entered his mind. The memory of the nightmarish episode hit him hard and his eyes painfully flew open. The realness of the dream disturbed him, leaving him feeling lost and helpless. A sensation he detested, believing that such feelings of inadequacy didn't belong to men.

Even so, the minor tidbit that bothered him the most was the simple fact that he had no clue as to the identity of the child. As far as Eddie knew, he was nothing but a killer -- father to no one.

But regardless of what Eddie believed, this one little child, continued to haunt him in his dreams. Nightly, she seemed to find him and visit him in one fashion or another. But all the dreams ended the same way. He could never get to her in time.

With consciousness, his mind began to clear and he quickly erased thoughts of the child. He began to believe she was nothing but a figment of his tormented imagination. Besides, Eddie had more pressing engagement to attend to. His main concern for the time being, was staying alive and away from the police.

In the midst of his thoughts, he drifted off to sleep again.

Soon, there was a loud pounding noise at the door to the room. Spooked by the nerve racking sound, Eddie reached for his gun, prepared to confront the noise maker with hostility, when a warm body stirred next to him. For an agonizing moment, Eddie Strange was confused and disoriented. He scrambled over the bed, searching for his weapon. The loud banging on the door wasn't helping his situation at all.

Naked, Eddie sat back on his haunches briefly ignoring the irritating thumping at the door. Meanwhile, he looked towards one of the two occupants that had been in bed with him. Before he could focus and get his mind to cooperate, the door burst open and a flood of hot sunlight filled the small room like a search beacon.

Eddie's eyes blinked rapidly as he tried to adjust to seeing with the full intensity of the sun blazing into the room. With dismay, he realized that if someone was there to kill him, he would be hopeless to prevent his own death.

A short fat man with prickly hair stood silhouetted in the doorway with massive arms folded over a hairy chest. The man said in a grave voice, "Look here, you goddamned freaks! You have thirty minutes to pay for another day, or you have your nasty asses off my property by 11 am. And if you need some fucking help, I'll get the cops to assist you."

Without warning, the room was cast back into darkness as the thin wooden door was slammed shut.

With sudden clarity, Eddie remembered where he was and who he was with. Now that his mind was finally on track, Eddie decided it was time for him to get up, find his gun and get dressed. But first, he needed to determine the sort of predicament the previous night of partying had left him and his guest in.

"Who the fuck was that?" asked one of the women who sat up sleepily in bed. Her name was Rochelle and she was what most black men referred to as an Amazon. Rochelle was the embodiment of dark chocolate that had been melted over a six foot, three inch frame of thickness and beauty, enhanced with 38-D sized breast. She had evil black eyes and a mouth as foul as any seasoned sailor.

"That," Eddie replied with a raspy voice, "was the motel manager. Fat fuckin' bastard came all the way up here himself to entice us to leave. See how much money we've got and then go pay that greasy mutha-fucka."

"Okay Baby," Rochelle said as she stretched her tall, flawless body. Within minutes, she was dressed and counting the money left out on the cheap dresser.

"We have about a hundred bucks," she informed Eddie with her back to him.

"Then pay for another day and bring us up some coffee," Eddie instructed her. "And hurry the fuck up," he added, "Cause if I see that fat man's face again, I just might kill him."

Without waiting for any form of acknowledgement from Rochelle, Eddie retrieved his Taurus .357 from between the mattress and headed towards the bathroom to shower and prepare himself for the day. Things were heating up and he needed to be prepared for the worst.

Excerpt from the soon-to-be-published novel "It's Hard Being the Same" by Eric Curtis"

CHAPTER SIX

BLACK

"You know homie, we need to come up with a way to cut this shit lose. All day yesterday we was running around collecting money so we could pay off these fools and make this next run up north," Black said.

"Well, what do you wanna do? We make most of our money on these trips," Yellow Bird replied.

"I know, but I'm about cool on this shit."

"Don't trip man, we'll come up with something. You been saving yo money?"

"Hell yeah, why?"

"I don't know, if we stop this we're gonna need something to make up for it. And you know them boyz ain't gonna wanna let us go that easy."

I didn't answer the homie, his words had me focused on the road. Before I knew it, we were in Bakersfield. My boy Voodoo was there waiting with the usual rent-a-car. Within its back seat there were fifteen kilos of cocaine, which was due in Sacramento in seven hours. I could make the drive in four hours and some change the way I drove, but riding this dirty could get a nigga on lock forever and a day. Before we hit the road, we made sure the dope was secure and that there was nothing laying around inside the car that would cause us to be arrested if we happen to get stopped.

Yellow Bird made sure the tags were good and that there was no broken tail lights. "Black, from what I can tell, everything looks good, the radar detector will have to do the rest. As long as you pay attention to it we should be alright," he said.

"Cool, I'm ready to push. Hey Voo, we should be back here by ten tomorrow, and back in Compton a few hours later. I want you to meet us at Rosco's Chicken &Waffles in Carson for lunch at 1:00," I said.

"Alright I'll be there."

It's Hard Being the Same

"Yeah nigga, and when you get there I'mma have a cool surprise for you."

"Yeah whatever nigga, just don't bring no bullshit."

"When have I ever put bullshit in the game? Oh yeah, if you ride yo bike bring an extra helmet."

"What for?"

"I told you, it's a surprise. I peeped game last Friday and I'm tellin' you, I got something for yo ass. We out my nigga."

About an hour after leaving Bakersfield, Yellow Bird's phone rang. "What's up Candy?" he said.

"Hey, where are you?"

"About half way to Sacramento."

"I just called to say thank you again for the roses you brought me yesterday."

"Don't trip, I'm glad you like them. Shit the way you was smiling, I might have to buy you flowers more often."

"You know the one thing I liked more than the roses?"

"What's that?"

"Seeing you."

"That's always a good thing."

"When will you be back?"

"We should be back around noon tomorrow. Why, you wanna hook up?"

"I might."

"Okay look, if do, I want you to do me a favor."

"What's that?"

"I want you wear some stone wash 501 jeans and a white t-shirt. Also I want you to make sure your jeans are one and a half sizes too small."

"Why is that?"

"No questions, just do that for me."

"Hey my nigga," I interrupted.

"Candy hold on a minute. What's up?"

"I was going to call Sandy, but tell her to take Sandy and Toni and meet us at Rosco's tomorrow afternoon at 2:00."

"Candy. Did you hear that?"

"Yeah I heard him."

"So you'll be there right?"

"Yeah we'll be there."

"Okay, just make sure you got them Levis on for me."

"Yeah whatever."

"Yeah you do that, and I'll call you tonight."

"Good. I like talking to you."

"You know I'm on a business run so I'll get at you later, K's up."

"Hey, I told you about that."

"Damn, I told you, force of habit. Bye!"

A few hours later we were in Sacramento with time to spare. G Parkway was our destination. A ten minute drive from the five freeway. It was surrounded by a rod iron gate with a guard station out front. Although they tried to clean this place up, this was still one of Sac's hottest dope spots, next to Del Paso Heights. Niggaz out here were still willing to pay $16,000 for every brick. If this shit work out today, we stood to make $240,000.

However, some bloods out of Oak Park wasn't feeling how two Compton Crips was makin' moves in their city. But little did they know we had six young niggaz staying in there. And we paid them real well to do one thing--dust anybody off that tries to interfere with our business. They know they are not to sell any dope, no gang bangin', all in all, no unwanted attention. And the $15,000 we pay them each month makes sure they comply with orders.

I called them five minutes before I got off the freeway, which gave them time to get themselves into position. When three Bloods saw my homie and I get out the rental with blue Kansas City Royal hats on, they thought they had some easy victims. "What's up blood?" One of them said. Yellow played it cool.

"Hey fellaz, how y'all doing?"

"Where you niggaz from?"

"Is there a problem fellaz?" Yellow Bird asked.

"Yeah nigga, I know y'all some punk ass Crips."

I moved over to the passenger side of the car with Yellow Bird.

"Check this out home boy, we don't want no problems and you don't need the problem we're gonna give yo ass," I said.

"Blood, you niggaz got to get up outta here."

"I plan to do just that in about fifteen minutes, so don't trip," I said.

"Nah my nigga, I mean now."

"You know what home boy, I told you we would push in a few minutes, after we handle our business. But see, yo ass want some shit you really can't handle. I'm tellin' you, be cool and we will do our thang and leave."

"Fuck that blood, you heard the homie," another of them said.

Yellow Bird took off his hat and threw it on the car, then he cracked his knuckles like he was ready to show off his boxing skills. One Blood looked like he was going for a gun, but before either of them could react, six heavily armed men came from three different directions. It was only four in the afternoon, but no one saw exactly where they came from.

Each of the killers had a 357 Desert Eagle in hand and a fully automatic Bush Master across their back. "Now check this out cuzz, you was saying we needed to get up outta here, right? We tried not to go there with you niggaz, but nah, you wanted to see how gang bangin' is really done. Now get yo punk ass on the ground. Six, pat these fools down for any weapons," I said. Only two of them had guns. "Four, we need something to move these dudes in."

"I'm on it boss."

"Yo Six cuff they asses with zip ties and get them ready to move. Yo hurry up, people are starting to take notice of what's going on." Just then, Four came up with an old school K5 Blazer, they loaded the trio in the back, and I told Six to go with Four. "Y'all go down to Carl's Jr. on Florin Road and wait for us. Make sure you park where no one will pay you too much attention, we should be there in like twenty minutes."

"I got you, should we air these niggaz out on the way there?"

"Nah nah, we got enough attention as it is. Hell I'm in a good mood, I just might let them go. Y'all push and we'll see you in a few minutes. Yellow Bird turned the car around while I opened the garage." As he did that, I told One to stand guard. As we unloaded the car, the rest of the crew faded back into their surroundings. Ten minutes later we were done and I handed One their pay for the month.

Things went well despite the run in with them Blood niggaz. I was still going over in my mind what I wanted to do with them. "Yellow."

"What's up?"

"You know we really need to make an example outta these niggaz.

But you know how I feel about killin'. We been doin' good on our runs."

"Yeah I feel you, but I don't appreciate them getting at us like that."

"Okay you make the call."

"I got this. One you got an extra car around here?"

"Yeah, give me three minutes."

"What's up?"

"We're gonna drive these fools to Modesto then have them walk home ass hole naked."

"That ain't bad."

"Yeah, well it will be after we put a bullet in one of their knee caps."

"Damn nigga, that's some cold shit."

"Cuzz, them fools will think twice about running up on some Compton niggaz next time."

After making sure everything was locked up, we all met down the road as I instructed. "Y'all did a good job. We were gonna push back to Compton tonight but tomorrow will be better. Besides we need the rest. One, I want you to search them again, make sure they don't have anything they can use to cut their way lose. Then go park the blazer in a place no one can see them. Leave them in there for the night."

"You punk ass niggaz get some sleep," Yellow Bird told them, "cause this might be the last time either of you wake up in the morning."

"Look, it's almost 6:00 p.m., y'all get comfortable it's gonna be a long night for y'all," I said.

"Damn boss, y'all some cold dudes."

"What, you want them to come sleep with you?"

"Nah, I'm cool."

"They can stay in the truck and you guys don't have to watch them for the night. You good with that?"

"Hell yeah."

"Cool, Six, here's what I want you to do, make sure both these cars are gassed up, go ahead and put these niggaz up for the night, then y'all go out and have some fun. We hit the road at 5:30 a.m. in the morning, so dress for the occasion. One, I also want you to bring two small caliber hand guns, but leave the rest of your hardware behind. We'll meet here in the morning. One more thing, I said loud enough for them to hear me. Bring a can of gas, I got something special in mind for these fools." They all laughed, and the three in the back begun to squirm and moan. We left and took off down Mack Road. Just past the freeway we got a room at the Comfort Inn.

YELLOW BIRD

After we got our things into the room, Black went out for food. With nothing to do I started flipping through the T.V. channels. When the porn popped up I started thinking about Candy, so I grabbed my cell phone. My shit actually got hard and it had nothing to do with what was on T.V.-- thinking about her in them Levi's did it. Damn, I should have gotten some bud from one of them young niggaz. Maybe the homie Black will come back with some.

With my shit still hard and frustration kicking in, I called her. "Hello."

"What's up sexy?"

"Who is this?"

"Oh you got jokes now?"

"Oh what's up Keith? What are you doing?"

"Sitting here holding my shit thinking about you."

"Damn nigga, what am I supposed to say to that?"

"You ask me that same question tomorrow when we hook up and I'll give you a real good answer."

"Whatever nigga. How did things go today?"

"We ran into some dudes from Oak Park, but they walked into a bad situation."

"You're alright though?"

"I'm talking to you ain't I? Look, what are you wearing?"

"Shit, you think your dick is hard now, if I told you, yo ass might blow a gasket."

"Don't trip on all that, now what are you wearing?"

"A lil of this and a lil of that."

"Why you playin' with the game?"

She laughed. "I'll tell you on one condition."

"What's that?"

"You gots to pay to find out."

"What I look like, a trick?"

"Hey, you the one that wanna know."

"Okay, how much?"

"I thought you would see it my way. It will cost you a C note for everything I tell you I have on then take off."

"Shit, with all the money I made today, I can handle that."

"Yo shit still hard?"

"Oh hell yeah."

"Too bad, I gotta go, here I come mom."

"That's fucked up Candy, you gonna play me like that? Wait until I see yo ass tomorrow."

"I can't wait, I love you too, Bye!" Damn, that was a first, I wonder if she really meant to say that shit?

CANDY

Damn, I hope he didn't catch what I just said. I don't know myself if I love him or not, but I know I can't wait to see him tomorrow. I could have easily played with myself just now while he was holding his dick, but that will have to wait. Although I haven't let him fuck me too many times, we have hooked up before and each time was off the hook. The way he seems to love eating my pussy was really making me miss him. I am so tempted to call him back, but instead I got up and went to my closet. If his ass wants to see me in some Levi's, one and a half sizes too small, the Apple Bottoms I'm gonna wear is gonna have that fool wanting to fuck me right through my jeans.

YELLOW BIRD

Black Bird came in with some Mexican food from taco Rico's. "Cuzz, why you watching that shit?"

"Man you don't wanna know. Check this out Black, I've been thinking and we need to go ahead and dust them three niggaz off."

"Where did that come from? You said you agreed we shouldn't kill them."

"First give me my food, I'm hungry. "

"Here."

"Good looking out. Look, the more I think about it, the more I realize that leaving them alive will cost us in the long run. Them fools saw too much."

"They've seen the drop spot, they've seen the hit squad we got stashed up in there, and they're gonna know we're protecting something of value. All in all, they just seen way too much."

"Cuzz, them niggaz don't have what it takes to fuck up what we got going."

"Maybe, maybe not, but even if that's the case, they will eventually talk about what went down today, even at the risk of embarrassment. If they don't come looking to check us out, someone else will."

"Man you seen how them young niggaz took care of business today? That's what we pay them for."

"Yeah, that's just what I'm talkin' about. If they have to put in major work in that lil ass area, eventually the police is gonna show up, and if there is an investigation, you can bet today will come up. If we allow that to happen, we're gonna upset a lot of people, so we need to do this."

"Okay Crip, you know how they say guns don't kill people, people kill people?"

"Yeah."

"Well I'mma prove them wrong, cause I'mma dump a whole lotta bullets into they ass." About thirty minutes later after taking a shower, I told Black to call or text One, and tell them to get here as soon as they could with the soon to be murder victims. "Tell them they only need the blazer and some hand guns."

"Man what are you talking about? I thought we were gonna take care of this shit tomorrow?"

"Shits changed. We were going to just hurt them a bit and send them on their way, but now they won't live through the night, and I plan to be in Compton when the sun comes up or very close to it. Now make the call, I'll be back in a few, I'm going to AM/PM to gas up the car. You want anything?"

"Yeah, to get some much needed sleep."

"Man yo ass can sleep in the car.

Excerpts from the soon-to-be-released novel "Penal Code Crimes" © 2007-2008 by Julian Glenn Padgett

CHAPTER 1

The Memory

The rain outside her upscale office building drizzled down her window in fine sheets. Having completed all of her legal motions for tomorrow's 402 evidentiary hearing, she kicked off her heels and began deciding her next move. At forty-eight years old, Natalie Prager was very beautiful. Standing five foot ten inches tall, she was a statuesque and gorgeous-looking woman. She had deep green eyes with flecks of brown just on the outside of her pupils. Her cheekbones were high and her nose turned up slightly above her mouth. Time had been good to her to the point that she could now conceal her pain behind those windows to her soul. The slight wrinkles she had around her eyes complemented her looks. Her lips were not as full as she would have liked but she refused to do the "Botox boogie" that her girlfriends participated in every two months. Her socialite friend, Peggy Miller, had done that procedure so much that her lips looked as if they were about to give birth to a whole new pair. *That woman never knows when to quit.* She laughed inwardly to herself. There was something about being stuck in the lips with a sharp needle three to six times every two months that never appealed to her sense of vanity. Although she had always wanted pouty lips like that late Negro actress Dorothy Dandridge, or that young black supermodel Naomi Campbell, She had resigned herself to the fact years ago that her lips would never be as naturally full as she desired. Being from a long line of "WASPs" she knew her chances of having a mouth like Angelina Jolie was not genetically possible.

Natalie made it a point to take her Pilates and Yoga classes three times a week. They kept her body long, lean and strong. The yoga centered her spirit and she always left feeling happy and rejuvenated. All of this, coupled with the treadmill at her law firm's gym kept her fit. But she still could not seem to shake her Krispy Kreme doughnut habits. "Ah well," she thought. "Can't have it all." Her body was curvaceous like a dancer's, and the same skinny and gangly legs that had gotten her teased so much as a little girl would now slow down and stop traffic with ease. Her breasts were not large but they were big enough for her size. And thanks to watching the *Oprah* show, at forty-eight, she finally knew how to shop for the proper bra size. Now that her face had lost all of its baby fat, she was finally beginning to think that maybe she was an attractive woman. Her aristocratic features were an obvious gift from her mother's side, never revealing her father's country white-trash background that she had worked so desperately to erase.

She was known in the legal circles of Texas as "The Hammer." After graduating from Houston University School of Law, she had chosen to be a prosecutor. It was there in those treacherous corridors that she honed her skills, and became the top prosecutor with the Odessa District Attorney's Office. For eleven years, right out of law school she had studied the gritty science of putting people in prison. They gave her the toughest cases and she always came through. Once she learned the game of law, her conviction rate had become legendary in the State of Texas.

However, after eleven and a half years with them, she had become burned out. She had seen way too many prosecutors and dishonest cops turn an honorable profession into a dishonorable battlefield. So, she had resigned after coming back from a four-month sabbatical. That time away had made it easier for her to make the career move.

It did not take her long to choose her firm, and when she had, they were off and running. Her corner office overlooked beautiful downtown Odessa. It was roomy with a large window that always invited her to witness some of the most beautiful Texas sunsets ever. A miniature waterfall she had purchased from the Nature Store stood off in the corner of her office. Its low gurgling sounds always relaxed her, especially after a rough day in court. Pictures of her children crowded her office walls in different areas. Natalie was the founding partner of her law firm, Prager, Jahns, and Ruby. They practiced corporate, securities, and criminal law. And the firm had just recently come off a small victory, by getting a faulty guilty plea reversed. It took her firm five years of wrangling with the appellate court. But they had established and proved the required elements and won. The Hammer had struck again.

During her earlier years, her colleagues had always underestimated her abilities. To them, she was just too attractive to be as good as she was. Some used the old rumor mill to assuage their insecurities, saying that she had slept her way to the top. Her close friends knew that was not true. Besides, she had a healthy sex life and she was sharp enough not to waste it on anybody she worked with. In reality, she had just been a smart deputy district attorney who knew the law and followed the evidence. Studying the Texas Penal Codes made her lethal. She was disciplined, thorough and cunning in the court room. Her philosophy was simple: "Trial is war. Win." And she used that philosophy to convict some of the most heinous individuals in Texas. Unfortunately, she lived in an age where women could not be great at their profession without having done something sexual to obtain their own success. A man could advance on his skill; a woman could only break the glass ceiling by being good in bed.

Her colleagues had that wrong too. She was not good in bed, she was great in bed. She knew from a young age that men wanted to be with her. And as she got older, she found women wanted to be her. And in truth, some of the men wanted to be her too.

She watched the sun creep down past the horizon as the rain continued to pelt her window. She inhaled the sweet aroma of the scotch in her glass. Then she fell back into deep thought. Many of her legal conquests had come because of men who had taken her beauty for granted in the courtroom. They were the ones who had found out much too late that, not only was she stunningly attractive, she was a force of nature.

As a natural-born leader, Natalie Prager was not afraid to get down and dirty. She had slugged it out with the old Southern-boy network that had dominated the halls of justice for years.

"You may not have liked me but you sure as hell respected me," she said to herself after taking a drink along with a bite of her Krispy Kreme old fashioned doughnut. She had proven her legal skills time and time again and was ready for more.

Looking out her window, she downed more of her scotch and walked over to her desk to look at her children's pictures. They were the one thing in her life that had always made her happy. Despite her mistakes and secrets, they were the best and brightest things she had ever done. At seventeen, her son, John Prager, was the captain of his high school football team in Odessa, Texas. And her daughter, Vanessa Prager, was about to graduate with honors from Dover High School. Natalie had married for station and not love. She had resigned herself to that fact years ago. Not that her husband, Baldwin Leese, had not provided her with a fairytale lifestyle. He had. He was eleven years her senior and was the most successful real estate developer in Odessa, and he loved her, in his own way. She had never been a very passionate woman, at least not with him. But she had always made sure that the intimate moments they shared were honest. She owed him that much.

Baldwin Leese came from a long line of old Southern wealth. His family had amassed its fortune from cotton and moonshine. And they had money. Years ago, after finding out about his mistress, she had questioned him so sweetly till it was vicious. Her tactics were utterly delicious, almost sinful. In one fell stroke, she had sealed her children's as well as her own financial future, just in case Baldwin grew a pair of Texas size balls and left her for his young tramp. True, she had her own money, but she felt a lot more secure knowing she now had some more of his too. Baldwin Leese's male menopause had cost him dearly.

Sitting in her custom-made leather chair, she poured herself another drink and gulped it down. Grimacing from the jolt it gave her, she followed it down with one more shot and two more bites of her doughnut. Licking the chocolate off her fingers, Natalie put the bottle back down and grabbed the letter from under her desk calendar. From the moment she read it, her heart leapt and she knew her life was about to change. Unclasping her hair tie, her long mane of red hair fell down slightly past her shoulders. She was one of those few older women who could get away with having longer hair and not looking as if she was trying to hang onto her youth. The letter was addressed to her married name but that did not matter. She happily recognized the handwriting and held it to her chest after she read it. Immediately it brought back certain memories of her childhood that she had fought furiously to forget. And special ones she desperately fought to remember.

The memory was of a little dirt clod of land, where she played in raggedy dresses with no shoes on dirty feet. Her daddy, Boss Prager, had a shack there in the bayous of Shreveport, Louisiana. It was her little hell and she wanted to forget all of it.

The memory of what he used to do to her during his many drunken stupors made her shake. She was a little girl, and had no way of knowing that the things he was doing to her were bad things. But something told her they were wrong, because when he would finish, she always felt dirty inside. Like her body would never be clean again. When he would come for her he would put his huge smelly hands over her mouth to stop her screams. Boss Prager was six three with an unusually high voice. He was fat and a local moonshiner. And he always smelled like catfish. He was naturally mean but his famous "white lightning" made him even meaner. And Boss liked to drink.

When these assaults would happen, he would tell her he loved her. She learned to just lay there while he would do things to her that no father should ever do to a daughter. The first few times it happened she fought wildly. He slapped her so hard that her ears would bleed. The first time he molested her was after he had come back from gambling. She bled then too. He had been drinking and had lost all of their money, which meant no food for a week. When it would happen she would just be still and float above her own body and watch herself be violated. Those defenses had allowed her to survive the brutal attacks by a monster that had called himself her father. Afterwards, she would cry herself to sleep. She cried a lot when she a little girl.

It took her a moment, but her focus went back to the letter in front of her. Opening it, she stared at the words for quite some time. All it read was "Nattie girl." She felt her heart leap because she had not been called that name in years. Her memories immediately soared back to the summer of 1978, to the back woods of Shreveport, memories of a boy that she knew loved her as much as she loved him. It was also a memory of the day her daddy died.

Will Cunningham was the great-grandson of slaves and he had known Natalie since she was nine years old. At eighteen, he was tall, six foot one with broad shoulders and tender hands. She loved his hands. And he was simply the greatest baseball player she had ever seen. In the spring of 1970 when they were both ten years old, he caught her father molesting Natalie behind her house. Will had thrown a rock that hit him in the head so hard, it opened a deep long cut in his forehead and knocked him out. That was the last time her father had ever touched her. "C'm on, Nat," he said, pulling her along in the evening air.

"Will, where we goin'?" she had asked, embarrassed and crying.

"To my Grandma Mattie's. I'm not gonna ever let him or anybody else hurt you again!" he said, wiping her tears as he hugged her. And even though they were both kids at the time, deep down inside she believed him.

Afterwards he took her hand and they ran to his house where his grandma hid her for seven days. That night before she went to bed, Grandma Mattie had made her a special meal of hush puppies, collard greens, fried chicken and sweet potato pie. For the first time in a long while, little Natalie Prager went to bed with a full stomach, feeling loved and happy. And despite her horrible ordeals that day, no tears touched her pillow as she fell safely to sleep. Grandma Mattie was seventy-eight years old then and had baby-sat many of the white and colored children in her small town of Shreveport. Besides, it was not unusual for Natalie to be at her house. She had been there many times in the past, playing with Will out in the back woods. But as a woman, even Grandma Mattie knew that the moment she saw Natalie and Will together, nothing and no one would keep them apart. She saw the edges of a deep love in them grow as they grew. Natalie's phone intercom flashed and she tapped the pulsing light. "Mrs. Prager? Dr. Hirsch is on line two."

"Rachel, take a message and tell him I'll call him back tomorrow at 7:00 a.m. sharp."

"Yes, Mrs. Prager."

Pouring another scotch, Natalie gave a voice command to her sound system and Celine Dion's greatest hits began to play. The lyrics of her songs immediately took her mind back. It was a hot day in the summer of 1978 when they walked back from Wallowbee creek hand in hand. Natalie was eighteen years old and she was three months pregnant. Dragonflies buzzed by and the smell of sweet magnolias mingled with the loamy scents of tall willow trees. The creek was their special place where they would talk for hours. She had taught him how to dance there, and he had shown her how to hit cans with a rock from sixty feet away. Will had been her first true love in every sense of the word, and she had been his. Hand in hand they walked back to her Aunt's Lila's house. Years ago her Aunt had taken her in, after Grandma Mattie had confirmed the sexual abuse Natalie had been subject to at the hands of Boss. They were walking the back trail when a blast from a double-barrel shotgun tore the bark off a nearby tree right next to Will's arm. The mouth of the weapon hatefully yelled. It "boo-oomed" angrily across the stillness of the bayou, its echoes tickling every bird's wings into flight. By sheer reflex, Will pushed her away into the cover of the high brush. Turning and clutching his left arm, he screamed in rage and pain from the splinters lodged there.

"I knew I'd get you. I just knew if I waited long enough I'd catch yo' black ass," Boss spat crazily in his high pitched voice. "You been out here doin' all kinda' business wit my little girl. Yo' ass is gon' ride the pine for this here!" he yelled, as he leveled his shotgun at Will's chest. The smell of moonshine whipped off his breath as he spoke.

The first rock hit him hard and high, right in the same exact spot he had been hit by Will years ago. The second one she threw was high and to the outside of his chin. Boss Prager dropped to one knee, with blood gushing from both the old head wound, and the new cut just an inch above his chin. She had thrown the rocks just as Will had shown her. She was relaxed and aimed at the largest spot she could. And at the last minute she snapped her wrist. It was wicked. Natalie launched those rocks so hard and fast that her arm made a whooshing sound.

Thwa-wap. "Aaaggh!" Thwa-wa-pap! "Aaaa-agghh! Quit, you tramp bitch!" he screamed at her as he began leveling his shotgun at her. But it was too late. Will had shaken off the pain and drove his shoulder into the man's side. The weapon flew out of his beefy fingers as his momentum took them both to the ground. Wrestling and punching at each other, they instinctively knew this was a fight to the death. Boss bit into Will's hand, causing him to loosen his grip. Then he slipped out from within Will's choke hold and came up with a sharp hunting knife from his boot and cut him across his chest. Howling in pain, Will jumped back and lost his footing on the slippery grass and fell. Holding the knife up above his fat head, Boss rushed at Will, hollering in rage, arcing the knife down towards his chest. Rolling to his left, Will got to his feet and dodged the killing stroke. Boss then turned and rushed up towards Natalie with his knife. The roaring sound that came from the double-barrel shotgun echoed through the trees, loudly bouncing and cracking off the air. She screamed as the man that was coming to kill her lay on his face with a gaping hole in his side. Rushing to her, Will reached out with a look of shock on his face.

"Give it to me, Nattie," Will said, staring in her wet eyes. "It's alright;

gimme the shotgun."

"He was gonna kill us. Will, he was gonna hurt you. I couldn't let him, I. . ."

"I know. Nattie girl. Sshh."

"Oh my God, I killed my father. I. . . I. . ."

Her voice trailed off into nothing as Will gently pulled the shotgun from her fingers and held her close. Before taking her home, he made her promise that she would never say a word that she had been there, or killed Boss. And through painful tears and wracking sobs, reluctantly, she agreed. It was dusk when they made it to her Aunt's house. Before he left he gently wiped her tears away then she kissed him softly.

"It's gonna be alright, Nattie girl," he said in a faraway tone.

"No it's not, Will. I'm scared and I know it's not gonna be alright. Will, ple-ease? I love you, we can figure this out. They'll believe me!" Natalie shouted between more tears and wiping her nose.

"No they won't, Nattie. You know they won't. This is the South. He tried to kill you!" he yelled.

"No. He tried to kill *us*," she said, reaching for his bleeding arm.

"I know that, but look at where we are. They'll put you away and we'll never see our baby again," he said to her. Natalie looked at him with a madness in her eyes that he had never seen before.

Through hopeless tears, he burned his point into the eyes of the woman he loved and the family that he would have. Falling down on both knees, he pulled her close, wrapped both arms around her waist and softly kissed her growing belly. He got up slowly and caressed her face one last time as a warm Louisiana rain began to fall. Grabbing his head, she turned it up to hers and saw the decision on his face that words would never give justice. And at that moment, her heart and the hearts she was carrying shuddered in depthless fear. "Will, no. Please baby no. No!" she pleaded desperately.

"I love you, Nattie girl," he said gently, prying her hands from his. Without taking their eyes from each other, Will backed away as the rain fell harder. Then he turned and ran, disappearing into the night.

"I love you too," she replied, watching as the rain stole his foot prints. Standing there between tears falling from her own eyes, and the sky, she found herself wishing the rain would wash away this horrible night.

Natalie had not thought about the details of that moment in decades. Now here she was with his letter and a tornado of endless thoughts bashing around in her mind. Tapping a button on her phone, she spoke softly into it.

"Rachel?"

"Yes, Ms. Prager?"

"Transfer all my calls to my voice mail please?"

"Yes, Mrs. Prager."

"Please get the limo ready." She clicked off before Rachel could respond. Then she pressed another button on her desk and the lights dimmed themselves. She sat there in deep thought and felt a thunderstorm brewing in the pit of her stomach. Her heart fluttered with unknown excitement, but the years had matured her senses. She was not the same person he had known all those years ago. And she knew he was not the same either. Her profession had shown what evils prison did to a man. She knew whatever it was, Will would not have contacted her after all these years unless he was absolutely sure there was some danger moving toward her. She went over the words in the letter one last time. "Nattie girl." Then she got up, put her high heels on, grabbed her purse and her Blackberry and headed to the garage of her office building, where the firm's limousine was ready and waiting.

Because of the rain it took the driver three hours to drive to Paddock State Prison where William Cunningham had been doing time. Whatever it was waiting for her, she was going to face it head on. She was not going to allow him to go through it alone, not this time. After all, she was not that scared little girl anymore; she had proved it time and time again. The one man in her life that she truly loved needed her help and she was going to move heaven, earth, and if need be hell to do it. After all, she was the great Natalie Prager, the hammer.

CHAPTER 4

So Long Ago

As Natalie rode down the interstate, Paddock State Prison loomed over the distance. It owned the expanse of land like the clouds above owned the sky. Even the clouds appeared to be afraid to float too close to its gun towers for fear of being shot down. Its architecture was formidable, like a fabled mountain that G-d formed when angels walked the earth with man. To her, its high spires licked the underbelly of the sky like an unwelcome lover. Instantly, unwanted memories of her father crept into her mind and she quickly pushed them aside. "Maybe that's why the sky is crying today," she thought to herself.

They turned left off the interstate onto Paddock Road, and in ten minutes they were driving into the huge parking lot of the facility. The wind rocked the black Town Car gently when the driver stopped in the large parking lot at the prison. The rain outside had slowed to a calming drizzle. Her love for the rain made this place just a little more bearable. She trembled slightly and questioned herself as to why. Was it a chill or because of who she was about to see, after so many years? But those thoughts abruptly faded as she stared at the monstrosity of a prison. "My G-d Will," was all she could say.

It stood off to her left like a hulking beast with an insatiable hunger to ruin. Subconsciously, she began picking at the thread in the limo seat next to where she sat. Anything to calm her nerves. The limo and its warm cushions were her comfort zone and she was in no way ready to let it go. Because she realized the moment she stepped out of it, whatever "this" was about was going to become very real, very fast. Fumbling with the mirror above her, it finally flipped open and the automatic light clicked to life. She brushed her hair and checked her make-up one last time. Natalie was so involved with everything else around her she never heard the window separating the driver from the passenger whirring its way down. It was the friendly voice of her driver Max Schell that brought her back to reality.

"Ms. Prager, you're gonna' have to get out if you're going to go in and see him. I'm pretty sure they're not going to let him come out here and sit with you," he said with a straight face. Laughing nervously, she smiled and said softly, "Ya think, Max?"

"What are you doing?" he asked, glancing at her in his rear view mirror.

"I'm checking my make-up."

"Why?"

"What?" she asked in an embarrassed tone.

"I said why are you checking your make-up when you're not wearing any?"

"Wha..? Oh yeah, I know, Max. I know." Her tone was far away like her thoughts. Max Schell was a sixty-eight-year-old retired Marine Gunnery Sergeant. They had known each other for what seemed like all of her life. She hired Max twelve years ago. He had been driving for her for eleven years now. He was five foot nine with a face like the marshmallow man. And he was absolutely the toughest man she had ever known. Everything about him was military. Max Schell was religiously consistent in everything he did. And that is what she admired most about him. He never let her down. He was the true definition of the word dependable. Sensing his concern, she looked up at him and smiled. Her hand whipped up and she quickly closed the mirror and the cab was once again bathed in immediate darkness-which was good, because her face was hot-house red with embarrassment. After all, this was only an attorney visit. . . or was it more? Did she want more? Did he want it to be more? "Hell, I don't know what this is!" she mumbled aloud to herself.

"So now you're talking to yourself?" he pushed again, still with a straight face.

"Whoa. No. I was just saying, Max." Before she could finish, he put up both his hands to stop her and smiled.

"Ms. Prager, I'm just trying to lighten your mood before you go in to that awful place, and do whatever it is you're going to do."

Lowering her head in the dark, she cupped her forehead in her hand and shook her head from side to side.

"Are you gonna' be okay, Ms. Prager?" he asked, turning back to face the front window.

"Yes, Max. Thanks for asking. I'm going to be fine. I'll see you when I see you."

She stepped out into a cold wet breeze that swept wisps of her red hair into her mouth. Kneeing her door shut, she turned and headed inside. Something or someone had set off Will's alarm. Whatever it was worried him enough to contact her after so many years. Weaving her way through the cars and trucks to the side walk, she took a deep breath and marched on. Onward to a future of unknown possibilities and to a destiny that she had been forced to give up, so long ago.

CHAPTER 7

Eyewitness to a Murder II

"Hello Mrs. Leese," came the deep gentle voice. Instantly, like lightening, she knew it was too late, and she hated him for that. Her head popped up, and wisps of red hair fell onto her right cheek. Putting her pen back in her purse she stood up, and with her thumb she mindfully tucked her hair behind her ear. After all these years, his voice still made her feel safe and warm. Here they were both in a prison; she was staring at a man she owed more to than could ever be repaid. It had been twenty years since she had seen Will and her heart was pounding in her chest and throat.

"Quit acting like a dizzy schoolgirl," she thought to herself, "It's only Will." She knew they both felt awkward, like two kids at their first Sadie Hawkins school dance, scared and unsure or maybe it was just her. She watched him as he stood there his coffee brown eyes drinking her in, she felt her left hand begin to tighten up which caused her to clench and relax her hand. Immediately she wanted to know what he was thinking but he said nothing. Will just looked at her.

"Stop that! She thought to herself; this is official business and you can't look at me like that Will." Immediately a thousand more questions fell into her heart, *"Oh God, What am I doing here, this was a mistake, does he feel as scared as I am? Why won't he say something? Damn it, I should have put on some lipstick or something."* Will was dressed in prison blues, his shirt and pants were dutifully creased, and his shoes were a shiny brown. To her they appeared to be brand new. Will gently grasped her right hand and shook it; she felt the warmth of his hand on hers and immediately pulled her hand away.

"This is a legal visit nothing more," she thought to herself.

Will's hair was cut short, close to his head. Nevertheless, she spied the small tight curls of grey hair coming in around his temples. Even some of his eyelashes were graying. The strong jaw line, high cheekbones and round eyes had not changed a bit. She could see no real differences in his outward appearance. But she knew that somewhere inside, Paddock State prison had changed him. How could being caged not change a man? Yet it was definitely her Will, she could not help but feel he was in there somewhere.

Backing away first, he extended his other arm, motioning her to sit down. And without taking their eyes from each other, they did. Suddenly she felt that everything was happening way too fast for her so she took in four breaths and exhaled each one silently. Letting go of his hand she placed her palms down on the table, and sat forward. Natalie did her best to look strong, but her eyes began to fill with tears. Crying was the one thing she was not going to do.

"Damn it, damn it, damn it!" she exclaimed in hushed tones. "I told myself, I wasn't going to do this in front of you."

"It's okay, Mrs. Leese," he said, putting his hands on the table too.

"No it's not," she said with a nervous laugh. Without a handkerchief in her purse, Natalie began dabbing underneath her eyelids with her fingertips. Leaning back, Will grabbed some tissue from his shirt pocket and reached out gently wiping her tears away.

"No," she said leaning her face away. "If the guards see you."

"Well, guess we have to make sure the guards don't see then, huh?" he answered, still leaning towards her.

"Stop that, Will, you could get in trouble for this," she said unconsciously, turning her face so he could wipe beneath her other eye.

"What are they gonna' do to me, Mrs. Leese? Put me in prison?" Will said, folding his handkerchief. His laugh was low and short but absolutely sweet to her ears. His gentleness was not helping her emotional state at all. She watched as he folded his handkerchief, leaving it cupped in his hands. Reaching forward she rested her hands in his on the handkerchief, then pulled them away.

As tragic and ironic as that statement was, it brought a small smile to her face. Seeing him today unearthed a woman that she had loved and admired, but let die ages ago, on a rainy dark night. It was that woman deep within her that she had suppressed with everyone over the years who knew her only as the Hammer. But with Will, she could still be vulnerable without fear, open, without the closed door of rejection; never berated, always beloved. Hurriedly she cleared her throat, made a sniffling sound, and composed herself. She was not going to be led around by her emotions. She was the Hammer, not some fool-headed girl.

"Well, Mr. Cunningham, my firm got your letter," she said in a rapid professional tone. Will looked at her with a knowing gaze and cocked his head to one side. He sensed her nervousness from the way she was rushing her words.

"You still do that," Will said to her, trying not to look bothered. Instantaneously, Natalie felt the heat of seriousness rise from him, like smoke from a once-dormant volcano.

"Do what?" she asked in a troubled tone.

"When you're nervous about something, you still speak really fast," Will said smiling at her.

"No I don't."

"Yeah you do," he replied slowly, studying her whole face with his eyes. As a lawyer, she had learned how to read people. It was her profession, after all, to gauge at any given moment if a witness was telling the truth or if they were lying. When they were embellishing or holding some crucial information back. Natalie had seen it all before and knew the signs of a person with something to hide. What was confusing her right now was that Will had shown none of those signs. Natalie knew that he had not lied, nor was he going too. They had never lied to each other, but she sensed strongly that something was wrong. She had not seen this man in twenty years. Yet here he was with a weight on his shoulders that was so obviously heavy that he could not hide it. She had given up so much and he had given up more than anyone could ever imagine or should have too. And now it was her turn to help him in whatever way she could. In law school, her professors had taught her to never ask a question without first being damn positive what the answer was going to be. Here she was, flying blind and completely out of her element and as usual, her curiosity got the best of her because before she knew it, she tilted her head and gave him that concentrated stare that he knew so well.

"What is it, Will?" Natalie asked, looking straight at him.

He abruptly stood up and took four steps away from their table. He wiped his face with both hands and scratched the top of his head. To her it looked like he was trying to decide how to answer her question. Then he turned to look at her. Natalie watched him; he was in deep thought as he walked back and sat down. His nervous blinking told her that whatever he was about to say had shaken him. The expression on his face could only be described as undeniable dread.

"Will. . .?" Natalie began; however, before she could finish her sentence, he said the one thing that she did not ever expect to hear.

"Somebody saw us, Natalie," he said clearly.

At that moment, the epiphany of that specific lesson from her professors closed in on her like a prison cell. It was just now, in this moment, that Natalie finally felt its truth. Because what she just heard had nailed the Hammer to the wall. It took at least two to three minutes before she opened her mouth to respond.

"Are you sure, I mean-Will?" Her words came out even faster now.

"Yeah, I'm sure." His tone was grave and poignant as he sat back down in his chair.

The lovely butterflies in her stomach had turned into animals of hollering fear. It took great effort for her not to scream at the top of her lungs.

"Tell me everything. Who is it? How did you find out?"

"Mrs. Leese, listen," he asked.

"Stop calling me that name. I hate that damned name." The realization of her words flew out at him with poisonous venom. Will stood there still as stone and surprised because whoever this person was talking to him now, he had never seen her before.

"Now tell me everything," she said. Her tone was grim, her expression far away. Now it was her who sat forward.

"There was an inmate here about a year ago. A 'wood'." The minute he used that word Will lowered his head and started shaking it.

"A 'wood'?" she said, looking at him curiously, not understanding the term he used.

"Yeah. Sorry. A white guy, a white man." He brought his head up slowly looking at her.

"It's alright, Will," Natalie intoned, holding out her hand giving him a reassuring smile.

"No. No it's not," he replied, looking up at her. His expression was all she needed to see. He had spent decades in prison and that one word had told him that the stench of prison had enveloped him. The moment he locked eyes with her, it was apparent that a part of who he had been, the young boy was gone. As much as he wanted to erase it, he could not, did not even know where to begin. It was so bad she could feel his fear.

"Go on," she said.

"I was at work in the metal shop about a year ago. And I heard these guys talking."

"Woods?" she asked for clarification.

"Yeah. Anyway, I hear this one guy talking about his old cellie bein' an eyewitness to a murder. I didn't think nothin' of it at first so I went back to my machine."

"This sounds like some prison fable."

"That's what I thought too, Natalie."

"What changed your mind?" she asked hastily.

"He said that his cellie saw the guy get shot."

"That could've been anybody anywhere, Will," she said, concentrating on his face.

"I asked the guy how old was his cellie and where was he when this happened?"

"What did he say?"

"He said he was about eighteen or nineteen when it happened. Then he said Kingsport, Louisiana."

"Kings Port?" Natalie asked relieved. "Kings Port is a whole city away from..."

She stopped speaking when she saw how Will looked at her, shaking his head.

"He was wrong, Natalie."

"What do you mean he was wrong?"

"I'm not finished. The next day I'm in the chow hall and there's an alarm. So I'm sittin' in the Black area. And the guy who was tellin' this at work is kneelin' close to my table. After the alarm stops he walks by on his way out and says he got it wrong."

"He got what wrong?"

Slowly Will moved his hands over to where he could touch hers. Then he pulled his away.

"He got the city wrong. It wasn't Kingsport, Louisiana. He said his cellie had told him it was Shreveport, Natalie. Shreveport, Louisiana."

"That's still not enough, Will."

"I know. Don't you think I know what this is doin' to you. Just hear me out. Before he left, he turned and said his cellie had told him the police had arrested some Black kid for the murder, and he didn't even do it."

"How did he know, how could he know, and what else did he say?"

"His cellie told him it wasn't a Black kid that shot the old man. It was a girl, a white girl." And with that, Natalie reached across the table and squeezed his hands as tightly as he squeezed hers.

About the Authors

Speech is one freedom that can't be easily denied. The authors met while being prisoners at San Quentin state prison in a creative writing class. Uncaged Stories was conceived by the authors as a way to raise money to get their stories out. They each have memoirs and novels they seek to publish.

Rahsaan Thomas is a native New Yorker who is new to the literary world. He uses writing as a means to share his stories, which aim to achieve change. By sharing his insights from the perspective of both being a victim and a perpetrator of crime, he hopes to breed understanding and tolerance. Uncaged Stories is his first published book venture. He is also a Sports Editor for San Quentin News. (See sanquentinnews.com)

Jeffery Little is a writer, journalist, paralegal, and legal clerk typist. Born in 1963, he was raised in Maywood, Illinois and moved during his high school years to San Diego, California, where he spent the majority of his life. It was relatively late in life that Little came to know writing as something he could enjoy. Since then he has also discovered that it is an excellent way to express his anger, pain and triumphs. Now Little writes urban fiction that is "a little more substantial and outside the box" than "the usual urban novel."

Eric Curtis is a creative writer from Compton, California. Known as the Hub City, Compton is notorious for urban street life. During his twenty years of incarceration, Eric discovered a love for the pen in writing classes with instructors like Zoe Mullery. Now he is using his innate and developed skill to tell tales about the city he was raised in. He has completed a trilogy about three young ladies who have dared to take on the streets, love and even the government in "It's Hard Being the Same", "It's Hard Staying the Same" and "Black Magic". He hopes to bring these and other completed, yet unpublished works to the world.

Julian Glenn Padgett (Luke) has been writing for several years. He is part of a creative writing class that has published three of his short stories in their yearly Anthologies. Luke is also a staff writer for the San Quentin Newspaper. Additionally, he can be seen at Marinshakespeare.com as one of San Quentin State Prison's many talented actors. Incarcerated for burglary, carjacking and murder, Padgett is on his 19th year of imprisonment. His immediate goal is to publish his legal thriller, The Penal Code Crimes. It's about a Texas powerhouse attorney named Natalie Prager and a battle to free her client while trying to outwit a killer who knows her deepest and darkest secrets.

Contact Us
uncagedstories@gmail.com

Rahsaan Thomas
SQSP T99595
San Quentin, CA 94974